The Blue Knight

Cast From Camelot Book: 2

By: M. Francis Lamont

The first thanks is, as always, to my own little princess; Morgan. Your
support and encouragement mean the world to me. I hope you follow your dreams to write
your own stories.

To my work family, at the store: Diane, Emily, Amber, Ana and the rest of the Geoffrey
crew and the FamJam, Darren, Kat, Chris, Liz, Jodi, Craig, Ashley, Randy, Bruce and Tracey, I
don't know what I would do without you all. The support, encouragement and bartending are
always exactly what I need when I need it.

My red pen team, Steffany, Kerri, Sarah, thank you for the constructive criticism and your
friendship. You are amazing women.

To "The Team": Lila, Hedda, Erin and Jessa. thank you, you keep me sane. Hedda I will miss
your creative vision.

Thanks to David, the beautiful man on the cover, I wish you well on your next adventure.

To all my readers and those who asked for Lionel's story, thank you for the support. I can't
wait to read what you think of the story.

Cover:
-Photography: Golden Czermak
-Design: The Unmasked Creative
-Model: David Cook

This book is dedicated to stepdads.

Those men who stepped up to fill the void of fatherhood and the ones who
added a second paternal influence to the lives of those special children.
Thank-you
"Any guy can be a father, but it takes a man to be a dad."

This is a work of fiction. Names, characters, businesses, places, events, locales, and incidents are either the products of the author's imagination or used in a fictitious manner. Any resemblance to other works of fiction, actual persons, living or dead, or actual events is purely coincidental.

Prologue:

"Arthur you cannot ask this of me." Liam said, pacing before the window. "Each of them stood by me when no one else would. I will not leave them to return to the table. Not if they are still banished."

"Not banished Liam." Arthur said, shaking his head. "Simply not invited to the table yet. I intend to extend the invitation eventually."

"Why not now? They are good men, good knights. Look how they helped with Caelia and brought Bedver to the courts. It is not their fault that he escaped before the trial." Liam was determined to stand by his men and see that every one of them was brought back to where they belonged. "What have they done that makes them unworthy?"

"Lucas, and Emrys are too young, they have done nothing of note. Saffir seeks pain then repents for it at the temples of the old gods and the new. He has an inner darkness that must be addressed before he can sit at the table."

"What about Lionel? You cannot object to him. There is no one more responsible, more educated, than he is." Liam said, squaring off with his friend, not thinking of him as the king.

"You have been distracted, old friend. Unfortunately, he has responsibilities outside your household." He tossed a letter down on the table in front of Liam. "You remember his father? Alexander?"

"The man was evil. The most dreaded instructor we ever had." Liam shook his head and picked up the letter. "It is hard to believe that a solid, kind-hearted man ever came from that household."

"Well, believe it or not Lionel has a sister that is now his ward, or will be soon." Arthur pointed at the letter. "Alexander is dying. He has requested to see his son and that Lionel take his sister into his care."

"That is going to be hard. He does not talk about the man at all." Liam rubbed a hand down his face. "Alright. I will send Saffir and Gerard with him. They were going to meet the twins from Gore and bring them to Redbourne. Lionel's home is on the way. They can leave him there and retrieve him on the way back with the twins."

"Will that be enough time for him to make peace with the old monster?" Arthur asked, handing Liam the letter.

"It will have to be. It is all the time he has."

Chapter 1

Days later in Sir Liam's office at Redbourne.

"I have no wish to return home. I do not care what my father says in his letters." Lionel said firmly, looking Liam in the face. "He can send my sister to a nunnery or have his own men escort her to Redbourne if that is what is needed. I want to join the hunt for Bedver after what he has done."

"You do not wish to say a final farewell to your father?" Gerard asked, joining the duo from the windowsill. "I despise my old man, but I still wish I could have one last talk with him."

"It took a decade or more, and many late-night drinking sessions, to change that wish from a string of vehement curses to wanting to speak to the old ghost." Liam chuckled.

Lionel rolled his eyes and tossed the scroll that was summoning him North back onto the table. They did not understand. They could never understand what it was like to be the son of Alexander of Scotsbane in Northumberland. The man's heart was as cold as the weather and his son had never been able to measure up to the hard, brutal standards set out by the lord and his circle of church clerics. At Redbourne he was considered straitlaced and rigid but at home they thought him wild and unmanageable. He was the wild and rebellious boy, the great disappointment. That was what saw him sent to the court of the king, to be taught proper manners and the discipline needed to become a proper knight.

Proper.

Lionel hated the word and all that it meant and yet he could not help but succumb to the pressure to live up to the expectations of a man that had not laid a hand upon him in more than a decade. A man that had never had a kind word for him outside the fighting lists and hunting grounds, and who still held his little sister all but captive in that house that was more like a prison. He was surprised that his father had not contracted a marriage for Fiona to the son of one of his friends, or worse, a man of his own generation simply looking to breed heirs with a girl of good bloodlines that was not allowed to refuse him.

What if he had engaged Fiona to one of those pigs? He would have to get the contract broken. Surely the king would help with that if Liam asked. He had offered Caelia, Liam's new young wife, the chance to walk away from the arranged marriage they were in. Surely he would make the same gesture to save an innocent young girl from marrying a man she could not love? He would have to convince Liam to speak to the king, without going home.

"I am not going. That is final. I will get things ready for Fiona and be prepared to undo whatever contracts my father may have signed for her, with your help Liam." Lionel said, turning to look at his leader and the blacksmith he suspected was or had been having an affair with the older knight. "He may have started talks to see her married off to one of his...disgusting associates. I cannot let that happen to my little sister. She is sweet and kind. She deserves better than that."

"If you can get her here before a ceremony of any kind I am sure that we can find a way to negate any contract made without her consent, Lionel." Liam said with a kindness in his face that made the young man wish that this man was his father instead of the monster that waited in the north. "You will still need to get there though. I am certain that a few of the men would go with you. You do not need to go there alone."

"I do not need to go there at all Liam. He simply wishes one last chance to torment me."

"Have you considered that if you do not go that he will take that anger out on Fiona?" Gerard pointed out, picking up the letter from the table. "You may hate the man, that is your right but to leave her to deal with him alone in that state would be a cruelty that I doubt the girl deserves."

Lionel hated that they were right, it was undeniable though.

He had to go home.

He had to go and bring his sister here, away from the hellish life he had left her to. Hopefully, she did not hate him for what he had chosen to do. If she did harbour resentment he would devote significant time to make up for it. Lionel could speak to Caelia, Liam's young wife, if she could find a place for her in the house. It was a large estate and it would be easy for Fiona to feel isolated without the welcome of the lady of Redbourne. Hopefully, the similar age of the women would help to bond them together because Lionel did not know what young ladies held interest in.

A knock on the door brought another scroll in the hands of a messenger.

"*Lionel,*

It has come to my attention that you might consider yourself absolved of your responsibility to me and to this family since your departure to Camelot. Let me assure you that I still hold you to all responsibility to me, this estate, and the name of your family. I hold you especially to your duty regarding your sister. If you fail to do as commanded then the entire property, your sister included, will pass to the church and my friends there. Her future, the fate of her innocence and happiness are in your hands Lionel. Do not delay."

His father had signed it with a flourish and sealed it with wax. It made Lionel feel as though a death warrant for his own happiness had just been put into his hands.

The old man knew how to play on his emotions. He knew that Lionel had left in an attempt to keep Fiona safe.

The affection between the siblings had always bothered the old man who had never loved anything or anyone, he simply wanted to control what he desired. When Lionel thought that his father would start to use the safety and well-being of his sister to manipulate him he had left with only a farewell letter on the pillow of Fiona's bed. Riders, letters and even priests had been sent by his father to attempt to coerce Lionel to come home, but he refused. He knew that there was no love behind the action, simply greed and the insatiable need to command those around him.

"Gerard? Will you come with me?" He asked the blacksmith with a sigh of resignation. "Perhaps Saffir as well? I will need someone who can manage the priests."

"I will and I am certain Saffir will as well." Gerard said, sharing a quick glance with Liam. "We are a brotherhood Lionel and will stand together as one. Whatever you need we will work together. You are not alone this time and we will make sure that he knows that."

Lionel had judged Gerard more than once for his past and even for some of the things he had done since their recent journey to Camelot. It was questionable at best. His loyalty was the complete opposite. There was nothing that the man would not do for those he cared for and the rag tag group of castaways at Redbourne were some of the precious few the burly man cared anything about at all.

"Thank you, Gerard. You have my gratitude." Lionel squared his shoulders and looked at Liam. "Will you excuse me to go gather what things I will need for the journey? If I am to do this I would like to leave at dawn. The journey will not be easy and that is simply the travel. My father will not have a warm reception for me, no matter who is with me."

"Get yourself ready." Liam said, picking up the scroll from the table. "I'll ask Caelia to see that some space is made for your sister. She will be welcomed with open arms to her new home."

"Thank you Liam. I appreciate it more than you know. She will blossom in the company of your wife and Hilda too."

"Elin will be here too." Gerard said, opening the door. "I will be going to Gore and bringing them both to Redbourne. We will stop to get the two of you on the way back so no one will be able to protest her traveling with only men."

Following the older knight across the great hall Lionel scoffed.

"I am sure that will be appreciated. Fiona has been locked away since I left. I have known nuns of the new religions that are allowed more freedoms than my sister has been afforded in recent years. Redbourne will be a whole new world for her."

"Is he really so bad as that?" Gerard said, looking over his shoulder. "He would keep her locked away simply out of spite for you?"

"It is not spite, but his need for control. Nothing scares that man more than not being able to direct each move of his children to his best advantage. That is the real reason he had children. We were to be his political pawns."

"But you left before he could use you the way that he intended?" Gerard said with a note of admiration in his voice.

"I left before he could force me to marry some girl that did not love me and fill that place with children that would have been born into a family that held no love." Lionel said with a shrug. "I had no wish to live that life. I know what it feels like to live with parents that do not love me."

"What about now? You can marry who you choose, with Liam's blessing and that of the king. Yet, you barely even danced with ladies at the ball in Camelot. Is there someone back home that holds your affections so strongly or, perhaps, someone that does not know of your affections at court?" Gerard asked, his face serious even though his tone was teasing.

"No, Gerard. I am not so unlucky in love as you are. There is no one that holds significance for me." Lionel shrugged. "I have never found anyone I could trust enough to take home and not be used against me by my father."

"Surely a woman of your own would not betray you to your father or allow herself to be manipulated?" Gerard said as they stepped out into the sunshine of the Redbourne yard. "I know that women can be fickle, but that seems extreme even for one of them?"

"One of what, Sir Gerard?" Liam's wife Caelia. "One of us women? I would have thought you had gotten over your constant misjudgments of my gender by now, or hoped at least that you would try a touch harder?"

Lionel offered Caelia a smile and raised her hand to his lips. The two of them had been through an ordeal in Camelot at the hands of Sir Bedver, the knight that had been behind Liam being removed from the Round Table on a false charge of rape. Since their return from Camelot Lionel had become close friends with Caelia and tried his best to help ease the strain that still existed between his leader and his young bride. He also kept encouraging a friendship between the blacksmith and the lady of the house, with nearly no results, not positive ones at least.

"I am certain that Ger did not mean to include you in that statement, Lady Caelia. A woman who can use a sword the way that you can is certainly unlike any other woman and should not be treated the same."

"I have to agree." Gerard said. "You certainly are unlike most women."

Both Lionel and Caelia could tell by his tone that he did not mean it as a compliment.

"Or, perhaps, you have no idea what women are actually like because...they don't like you." Caelia said to the blacksmith with a smile before she left them both behind to go into the house, likely to find Liam and hear about the impending arrival of Lionel's sister and the Royal twins from Gore.

"Well, Gerard, she is not wrong." Lionel chuckled, forgetting his angst for the moment.

"It goes both ways, my friend, it definitely goes both ways." The blacksmith laughed and headed towards his smithy. "I'll pack tonight so that we can leave in the morning."

"Yes, in the morning." Lionel sighed. "Scotsbane within the fortnight. Fiona and my father. Time to say good-bye at long last."

Chapter 2

Lionel was fidgeting with his horse's main while Liam reminded the three knights what it meant to be escorting the royal twins of Gore back to Redbourne and how important it was for the relations between their father and Camelot that things go well there and on the journey back. Lucas, Emrys and Rion were leaning against the wall, casually watching Lionel, Gerard and Saffir with a hint of envy that Saffir had been chosen to go on the first mission since Liam had been reinstated to the round table by King Arthur.

"I know that they are our friends, but they are royal ambassadors as well and should be treated as such." He looked at Gerard who could barely contain his grin. It was not known to the trio staying at Redbourne, or Saffir, that Gerard had a special relationship with the Price of Gore. Caelia did, which likely meant that Liam knew as well, but Lionel had seen the nature of their relationship with his own eyes. It was the kind that would horrify the king of Gore and his own father. They did not believe that there could be love between men in the same way that there could be love between a man and a woman. They agreed with the teachings of the new church, which preached that it was a sin outside the nature of God.

Lionel was not sure what he thought of the secret relationship between the prince and the blacksmith, it made him uncomfortable, feel awkward, but he would keep the secret. It was his duty as a knight and his honor as a brother to do so. He would never tell a soul outside the brotherhood of outcasts at Redbourne and even they would only know if they absolutely must.

Saffir would know by the end of this journey unless the two men had learned to act with some discretion.

"There will also be a special, new member of our household returning with Sir Lionel. His younger sister, Fiona, will be returning from Scotsbane to live with us here. I expect that you Gerard, and you Saffir, will make every effort to help Lionel get her here safely where the rest of us will do our best to make her feel welcome in her new home."

Caelia, who had come to join Liam gave Lionel a smile.

"I am looking forward to meeting your sister. I am sure that Hilda and I will be able to make her comfortable right away. Princess Elin will be a delight to have here as well. We have promised each other a duel and I have been practicing."

Liam kissed her cheek, Gerard frowned, rolling his eyes and Lionel laughed.

"I cannot wait to see that match. On that note, we should depart if we wish to arrive on time."

He nodded to Liam and the other knights then turned his horse towards the gate. It would take days to get to Camelot and than at least a week to get to Scotsbane. Most of a fortnight to be worrying about what he was walking into when he got home but less than a fortnight before he had to face his father for the last time.

It was an eternity and barely a moment at the same time. How did you prepare for the end of the life of a man that never loved you in the space of only a few days? What about Fiona? What if she loved the old man with the simple affection that a daughter had for her father? Was he prepared to console her in the midst of his own grief that was sure to be complicated?

He did not have an answer, not yet.

Lionel was not even sure that he could believe that his father was truly dying at long last but there did not seem to be a way to get out of this command to get Fiona, so he had to go. It would be wonderful to see her again after so long apart. That did not mean that he thought, for even a second, that he was going to enjoy this sojourn. There was certain to be torture, in the verbal form at least, from the second he arrived right until the moment his father left this world. At least he might be able to take some of the pressure off his little sister.

"Lionel, we are to ride North, not South." Saffir's voice cute through his thoughts to pull him back to the present. "Where are you going?"

He looked around to realize that he had turned in the wrong direction as they left the gate. Even his subconscious rejected the idea of going home. This could not be a good idea.

"Apparently the horse is reading my mind and trying to take us to the coast instead of home." Lionel faked a smile and turned to follow Gerard on the road North. "The beast is smarter than it's masters I think."

"In some cases that does not take much." Gerard said with a smirk. "So, tell us what we're walking into up there Lionel."

"Yes." Saffir joined the discussion. "You never talk about your home and I had no idea that you had a sister. Is she pretty?"

"She and I have the same blue eyes, from my mother. Other than that, singular thing, I resemble my father and she is the image of my mother, as much as I remember." Lionel shrugged. "That was her blessing and her curse while we were growing up. My father never raged at her the way he did at me, but he expected her to be exactly like my mother, which she never could be."

"He took his frustrations out on her?" Gerard asked with sympathy of a man that understood first-hand.

"He would have if I had not put myself between them until she was old enough that he could see her value to him. That was when he turned every bit of his rage against me."

"You are his heir though? Why would he work so hard to alienate you if he needed you to take over the estate and his title?" Saffir asked, pushing his long dark hair out of his face, and looking at Lionel with complete surprise. "You are his heir are you not?"

"As far as I know there are no others. My mother was the only woman he ever married, though I am sure there were others before, after and likely during that relationship." Lionel said with a hint of shame in his voice, even though the dishonor was not his but rested solely on the shoulders of his father.

"Your sister, is she going to be alright? Leaving all of the things she knows behind? Does she know that she is coming back with us?" Ger asked, looking over his shoulder at Lionel.

"No. I do not think she does. She has not written to me, which is a surprise since my father is so determined to get me there as soon as possible."

"The two of you are close then? Or were?" Saffir asked, with what sounded like a note of disappointment in his voice. "You expected her to write to you? Asking you to come or warning you not to?"

"We are still close, or so I assume. Which means that she is off limits to any man with courting, or similar thoughts on his mind." He made sure to maintain eye contact with Saffir with the last words. With his dark coloring and longer, wild hair, it did not take much more than a wink and a smile for the man to attract women wherever they went.

"I would not dream of such a thing Lionel, though I could not say that I would object to her advances either, should she make them." Saffir teased then rode ahead before Lionel could hit him with a mostly friendly punch to his arm.

"If I catch the two of them together I will advance him right towards the grave." Lionel muttered to Gerard.

"He is just teasing you. I doubt that Saffir would do anything to damage your friendship and he would certainly never dishonor your sister. The penance he would force upon himself for that would nearly kill him." Gerard shook his head.

"Then we are all in agreeance that any man of our troop that interferes with my sister will die. I like that we are in such agreeance Gerard. That does not happen often." Lionel said, his voice heavy with sarcasm

They both knew that Saffir was a firm believer in physical punishment for whatever sins he committed. His back was covered in scars to prove that despite his religious devotion he still sinned. The worse the sin the harder the man lashed himself, which meant a deeper wound. He would not allow Caelia or even Helga, the matronly cook of the estate, to tend to the injuries and he never spoke to any of the knights of what his sins were. He was a mystery, even after the years they had all spent together in banishment.

No matter how hard he would punish himself for it, Saffir would not be allowed to 'sin' with Fiona. At some point Lionel knew that he would have to either find or approve of some man for her to marry, but the idea that it might be one of his friends was not something he could stomach. In his mind she was still ten years old, following him around because there was no one else to talk to. The concept that she was not only old enough to be married, but that some of her friends were already parents, was so far fetched that he was beginning to wonder if he would even recognize his sister when they arrived.

"If you two are willing to stop chattering, we could ride a little harder. We might be able to skip the roadside inn and make it to Camelot tonight. It will be late, but I would think that Liam's name would hold enough sway at the gate to get us admitted for the night." Saffir called from just ahead of them on the road. "I know that we cannot go to the palace without invitation, but we can go to the city itself at least?"

"You have never been banished before have you Saffir?" Gerard said, pulling his horse to a stop next to the young knight. "We will stay at the same inn that we did when we went with Liam to Camelot. Tomorrow we will ride around the edge of the city, after reporting to the guard at the gate why we are near the city. We are not invited within the walls of Arthur's capital unless it is an emergency of life or death."

"I am fine with that." Lionel said, nudging his horse past them. "I would not like to repeat all of this before the king and his councillors. It will be bad enough if there is a marriage contract that needs to be nullified. I do not want to expose all of this until it is resolved, and we are on the way home with the girls."

"Girls?' Gerard asked. "I thought it was just your sister that we were bringing back, as well as Elin of course."

"You really know nothing of women at all do you Ger?" Lionel chuckled. "She will have a handmaid with her, either Moira or Lilith, and they will be coming together. You do not separate a woman from her friends."

"Caelia did not come to Redbourne with a maid." Gerard countered. "She is the wife of a knight and the daughter of one. Why did she not bring someone with her?"

"Because her father did not have one to send with her and she is unlike any other woman I have ever met. You cannot hold her to the same expectation as most of the noble ladies."

Saffir nodded his agreement.

"She's different. What do you remember of these girls your sister might have with her?"

"Moira is the daughter of my father's right-hand man and who I was supposed to marry. I refused to sign the contract though." Lionel said, trying to keep a calmness in his voice that he did not feel.

"I am going to guess that had nothing to do with the girl and everything to do with your father and the fact that he wanted it?" Gerard said with a nod.

"What about the other girl you mentioned? Lilith?" Saffir asked. "Who is she?"

"Lilith?" Lionel shook his head. "Lilith is trouble."

Chapter 3

Lilith was in trouble, again, or she was going to be if Sir Alex saw this mess. The shattered glass of the jug and the wine were all over the floor. Even if she got it cleaned up before he saw it someone, probably Moira, was bound to mention it to him. If she were lucky it would be late enough at night that she could leave her daughter in bed and deal with the old knight herself. If Fiona were nearby she would certainly do her best to help but there was only so much the other woman could do to calm her father. Without her the elderly knight's temper would be monstrous, but at least he was too frail now to be physically violent.

"I dinna mean to mama." The small voice of Elaine said mournfully from the doorway. "I just wanna be a helper. Then you can play more."

"Oh, my darling. I wish that were the case. I know that you get lonely in this big place, but I work hard so that we have a place to live that is warm and safe for both of us." She said, crouching down to wrap her arms around the tiny shoulders. "I will come and sing for you though, before bed, if you get up to our rooms and wait for me there."

"Bring suppers?" Elaine's small face lit up. "Warm bread and the good butter?"

"The best butter in the whole place. Now scoot on upstairs. I will be there as soon as I can."

The tight hug and the wet kiss pressed to her cheek were worth all the stress of dealing with the judgments of the town and, loudest of all, her employer. When she had found herself pregnant four years ago, Sir Alex had assumed that the father of her unborn child was his son and it had taken a lot of convincing to assure him that was not the case. He had screamed and threatened all manner of violence against her. He even went so far as to bring the Sheriff to the manner and tried to have her arrested. Still she would not name the man responsible, only stated that it was not Lionel. The old man was livid, especially when the Sheriff said that there was nothing that he could do. Since Lilith was not trying to extort money from the family or trying to force Lionel to marry her, there was no crime and no need for his services. The old knight had threatened to have the sheriff dismissed from his office, but the man told him that the law was the law, it did not matter who was reading it. Once he was convinced that his son had nothing to do with her condition Sir Alex ceased to care unless he could use it to hurt or control her.

Lilith had never told anyone who Elaine's father was, which made it difficult for the local priests and farmers wives to force her into a marriage she did not want. There were many nights that she wished that there had been someone at her side to hold her while she cried, or someone who could have helped her through the angst and tantrums, but she had done it alone.

That was exactly how she intended to continue living her life and raising her daughter. Alone.

Nearly every friend that she had that were married complained to her constantly about their husband. The men were either neglectful or too demanding, some were even violent and nearly all of them were unfaithful. One husband was even unfaithful with another man, which was considered to be one of the greatest sins possible, according to the new religion that Sir Alex had brought to the area.

Lilith thought that the new church was simply an attempt to subdue the old ways that did not acknowledge the power some of these knights and lords tried to wield over the land and the people who had always lived there. The rules and morality that these priests tried to enforce were abominable and their punishments were beyond cruel. She was surprised that they had not forced her to have Elaine in one of their 'convent' homes and steal her away to pretend that some barren, noble woman had given birth to her instead.

It is possible that they would have done something like that if Fiona had not invited her in at Scotsbane and taken a stand against her father. She had never seen her friend stand up for anything like she did for Lilith, even Sir Alex was so surprised that he did not fight her on it. That was how Lilith and, eventually, Elaine, came to live in the attic of the manor of Scotsbane. To some, like Moira, it might seem shabby and dreary, but to Lilith it was a palace all her own once she got upstairs. No one bothered her up there amongst the cast offs and old furniture and she loved it.

It was her sanctuary and she would return to it as soon as the mess was cleaned up. If she was not found by the master of the house.

"I think that is all of it." Lilith said, getting up from the floor.

"All of what." The raspy voice she dreaded, called from the doorway. "What did you take now?"

Lilith looked up as Sir Alex slowly hobbled into the room. Leaning heavily on his staff and breathing hard the old knight was still a formidable man who now used his words instead of his sword to cause mortal wounds to those who crossed him. In some ways it made him more dangerous than if he had steel in his hands.

"As I tell you each time you say these things, Sir Alex, that I have not and never would steal from you." Lilith straightened herself and faced the old man as boldly as she could. "If you would care to remember I have, in fact, stopped people from stealing from you on more than one occasion. There was simply a spill and I wanted to make sure that it was cleaned up entirely before I retire for the night."

"You were not needed to stop anyone from doing anything, except that child of yours running around, screaming at all hours." He grumbled, scanning the room carefully.

"We both know that Elaine is a quiet child, Sir Alex. I can promise you that nothing is out of place in this room. Do you need help to get in your chair?" She walked to the end of the big dining table and pulled back his big throne like chair.

"Moira is coming with my supper. You can go." Alex waved his hand with an annoying dismissive air.

"I am right here, Sir Alex." Moira said, brushing past Lilith as though she weren't there. "Let me get you comfortable."

Sir Alex grunted as he let the thin, fair-skinned, dark-haired woman with a nearly scandalously low-cut dress ease him into his seat.

Lilith turned to leave, she and Moira struggled to remain cordial at the best of times and Lilith was too tired to ignore her barbs tonight. She stopped though when the knight called her name after his plate was put on the table.

" Lilith, I have something to say before you go and while Moira is here. It will save me the effort of saying it twice."

Holding back a sigh, Lilith turned to face the old man as he spoke.

"I have just received word that Lionel is returning to Scotsbane. It took me years to convince him, but the ungrateful brat is finally coming home to see me die." He watched both women carefully for a moment before continuing. "Neither of you are to throw yourself at my son. As much as I want him married and producing legal heirs to take over this place, neither of you are of the quality that I want adding to my bloodline."

Lilith stared at the man for a moment, stunned at the rudeness and the audacity that he would assume that either of them would have lowered themselves to begging to marry Lionel. When he had left, years ago, he had been a scrawny, bookish, prude. Only caring about rules and accounts and getting away from the North. She knew that he had slept with Moira, at least once, and though the other woman liked to throw it in her face at times Lilith had very few good memories of Lionel after their early childhood years.

"I am as likely to try to marry your son as I am to steal from you, Sir Alex." Lilith said, shaking her head. "I have never, ever, had any interest in your son. Now if you will both excuse me I have other work to do."

She turned on her heel and exited the room before either of them could say another word. Moira would be fawning over the old man, trying to convince him that she was worthy of his pious heir. At least it would be better that she tried to trap the son than continuing to chase the father on the way to his deathbed. It was disgusting to watch and, perhaps, formal Lionel, as annoying as he was, would be able to put a stop to the attempted lechery of their former friend.

"Oh heavens, I hope he can manage her with more intelligence than his father, that is if he can still think with his brain instead of his cock." She muttered to the ceiling while she walked down the hall towards the door to the attic and the refuge of precious moments with her daughter before the night's end.

"Who are you speaking of Lilith?" Fiona asked, stepping into the hallway on her way to join her father for dinner.

"Moira, as usual. Your father has just told us both that your brother is returning home."

Fiona's face burst into a smile.

"Lionel? Coming home at last? That is a blessing." She said, taking Lilith by the hand while they walked together. "I will finally be able to get out of this place and see Camelot. Perhaps we will go to Redbourne in the south and I will be able to be warm with the assistance of a fire."

"Perhaps we might both be free of Moira and her schemes to obtain a title." Lilith said, rolling her eyes. "That is what your father addressed just moments ago actually."

"My father spoke of my departure? I would have thought from the look on your face that he had mentioned who it is that he has betrothed me to." Fiona said, sounding nervous and with good reason. There was not much of a chance that Sir Alex had arranged anything that could possibly make his daughter happy.

"He has entered you into a betrothal without telling you who you are to marry? Is that even legal?" Lilith asked, stopping her in the hallway. "I thought it was monstrous when he told Moira and I that we were not good enough to marry his son. Who would he think is good enough to marry you?"

"He said that, to both of you? That you were not good enough for Lionel? He should be so lucky as to catch your eye. He is such a stickler for rules and proper conduct or was when he lived here at least. I should not wonder if he has gotten duller and more bookish with each passing year."

The two young women shared a laugh until Lilith said with a sigh.

"Yes. That is what he told us both. That we were not good enough to be adding to his bloodline. I left before Moira could speak but made it quite clear that I have no intention of getting involved with him. I will, of course, come with you wherever it is that you go from here."

"I am sure that Moira's head almost came off all together. That woman wants a title so badly I am surprised that she has not taken one of these old men that my father has been shopping my dowry around to." Fiona said, as they approached the dining room once again.

"Perhaps that means that he has not yet chosen one, so she does not know which to throw herself at yet." Lilith suggested.

"Then I pity my poor brother, because my father's words will mean very little if Moira decides that she wants him." Fiona said with a smile before joining her father and the other woman, in the dining hall and leaving Lilith alone once again.

"Yes, poor Lionel if she wants him, again." She said to the walls as she made her way back to the attic. "Poor Lionel indeed."

Chapter 4

Lionel was sitting staring at the remains of the fire in the dining room of the inn with a pint of mead getting warm in his hand while he watched the flames dying down to embers. Gerard and Saffir had retired hours ago and he had checked on the horses just before ordering the drink in his hand. The room had slowly cleared as, one-by-one, the crowd had dispersed upstairs or out the front door, leaving Lionel alone with his thoughts and the barmaid.

He noticed the woman watching him with all the subtleness of a barn tabby stalking a mouse. She was thin, almost skinny, with big blue eyes, shiny hair as yellow as stalks of wheat and breasts that needed the corset only to enhance the curves, not to hold them in restraint. Most nights he would have been amused. He might have even encouraged her attention if his mood had been better. Tonight, he could not decide if he wanted to be alone or if he wanted to pick a fight. Since she was the only person in the room the idea of a fight was not an option. It would not become him as a knight to pick a fist fight with a woman. The look in her eyes suggested that there might be another form of physical activity that would allow him to take out all the aggression coursing through him at the thought of dealing with his father in a few days.

"Do you need anything else from the bar sir?" The young woman said, the firelight sparking in her blue eyes. "Anything at all?"

She leaned over to take his empty cup that he did not remember drinking and gave him a delightful view of her bosom. The true offer, though unspoken, was crystal clear.

"Do you have any suggestion on how I could wear myself out enough to fall asleep within the hour?" Lionel asked with a dark smile. "I have some pent-up frustrations that are keeping me awake."

"Well, I could suggest a stronger drink or physical exercise." She said, perching the curve of her backside on the arm of the chair and placing a hand on his shoulder with a suggestive squeeze. "The exercise would be nearly certain to do the trick."

"I do not think that running around the outside of this inn is going to help me sleep." He said.

Lionel let his hand rest on the curve of her hip, his thumb stroking the linen of her skirt absentmindedly.

"Do you have any other suggestions that might see both of us to a good night's rest?"

"Well." The girl said, sliding off the arm of the chair and into his lap. "I think that the best way, the absolute best way, for us both to get a good night sleep would be to exercise together. That way you can make sure that I do not get hurt and I can make sure that you are utterly exhausted and sleep the rest of the night."

He turned her on his lap to straddle him and ran his palms up her thighs, bringing her skirt up with the same motion.

"You want to exhaust me? Work us both into a fever-pitch so that we collapse in our beds to enjoy the dreamless sleep of the passionately exhausted?"

"That is exactly my plan." She purred with a smile then leaned down to kiss Lionel on the mouth. "No one is around. You do not even have to move from the chair."

"Oh, really?"

She nodded and reached to unlace his breeches. Slipping her hand inside she took him in a firm grip and stroked him from tip to base and back again. The pressure was amazing and just what he needed to take his mind off his home and everything waiting for him there. Her position also put her breasts at the same level as his mouth.

Lionel reached out to take one in his hand. It was like holding a large, beautiful apple in his hand. She fit delightfully in his palm and moaned softly when he flicked her nipple back and forth with his thumb. It took no more than a simple tug to bring her flesh to his lips so that his tongue could continue the work of his hand. All the while her hand had continued to work his cock into a hard, throbbing spearhead.

"I think, if we are going to enjoy that sleep you spoke of to its full potential we should get that exercise started as soon as possible." Lionel said, letting her breast fall from his mouth to swing away with a glisten of moisture on its peak from his tongue.

"Yes, m'lord knight." She smiled and caressed the back of his head, pulling his face to her chest. "I will see you well taken care of tonight."

"Lionel. My name is Lionel." He said, running his hands from her shoulders to her backside. "Are you sure that this is what you want? I cannot promise you anything other than tonight."

"I do not want anything other than tonight." She whispered back as she tugged his trousers a little lower. "My name is Daisy, in case you want to remember it, Lionel."

She rolled her hips against his erection, teasing him with her nearness and stimulating herself in the same motion. He loved her boldness and confidence to take what she wanted when she wanted it. Daisy certainly was not like the shy country girls around Redbourne or the falsely modest ones in Camelot. She reminded him, a little, of the women near Scotsbane. Moira and Lilith were both flirtatious and fun, though it was with Moira that he had spent his first night as a man.

As Daisy threaded her fingers through his hair Lionel wondered if the girls of his childhood were now like the woman grinding against his cock or had they grown up to be demure women of the gentry who were now married with a brood of children?

"Lionel? Are you here with me?" Daisy said, feathering his forehead with kisses and gripping his shoulders while she slid up and down his cock. "Did you change your mind?"

"No. I am here. I am right here with you." Lionel said, brushing away a lose strand of hair.

"And I am here with you." Daisy said, shifting her body to hover above the tip of his cock. Placing her hands on his shoulders she eased herself down his length. "All the way here with you."

Sheathed within her heat Lionel found that there was nothing else that he could think of except for her body moving on top of him. His mouth found her neck and his hands grasped her breasts and her hip, grinding her harder and deeper against him. She giggled delightedly when he gave a quick pinch to her bottom but then their eyes met and suddenly they became much more serious. There would be no other night than this one. No sweet kisses or tender embraces, all they would have were these moments to create a memory and nothing more.

No one could know of tonight. Lionel had a sterling reputation when it came to women and relationships, which he did not want questioned. More important than his own reputation, however, was the damage that gossip and slander could cause the woman riding his cock with all the abandon of a woman who knew how to find her own pleasure. He was more aware than most men the heartbreak that could come if a woman were found to be sexually active before she was married. It was almost as bad as if she were to cheat on her husband. Society would be quick and brutal in blaming a woman while rarely condemning the man at all.

The fact that his leader, Liam, had been cast out of the court of Camelot for the liaison Sir Bedver had tried to portray as a rape instead of a willing night of passion between the senior knight and the young woman had been an amazing use of law and public opinion twisted for malicious purposes. None of the company had ever bothered to find out what had happened to that particular young woman, until they had returned to the city at the summons of the king. What Lionel had found out was shocking despite it being predictable.

"If you're not interested I can just go." Daisy said, interrupting his thoughts. "I have never been with a man that was so distracted. Am I doing something wrong?"

"No. I am the one doing something wrong." Lionel said, lifting her from his lap so that he could stand. "We should not be doing this. If anyone were to find out, your life and livelihood here could be damaged."

"No one is going to find out. You are sweet to show concern though." Daisy said, catching his hand and holding him back from leaving the room. "No one else is awake Lionel. Do not leave this unfinished and me wanting more, please."

He paused, his brain battling with his lust. She was right about their solitude and there was no doubt that he needed the release that she was offering through the passion of her body. It was an agonizing choice.

"Say that word again." He said, dropping his voice to a husky growl. "Say please."

A smile slowly spread across her lovely face and she tugged his hand again.

"Please, Lionel. Stay a little longer."

The simple words of request were all that he needed to hear.

A quick tug of her arm had her crushed against his chest. One arm wrapped around her shoulders allowed for a free hand to raise her skirt while he walked her backwards until she bumped into the edge of one of the tables.

Their tongues dancing Lionel eased Daisy backwards until she was laying across the worn planks of the bar table. With her skirt raise to her hips the fair curls above the slick and glistening pink of her core provided a gold-hued invitation for him to finish what they had begun.

"Just a little longer, pet." He said stepping between her legs, running his hands down her thighs. "A little bit longer."

Daisy nodded, bringing her hand down so that she could play her fingers through her curls to rub herself with a hungry enthusiasm. It was a beautiful sight, erotic and arousing. His blood was pounding through his veins, straight to his cock. He was hard and pulsing once again.

Gripping her thigh and pressing it towards her chest, Lionel leaned forward, penetrating her core with a slow pressure. The agony was blissful and excruciating. Each thrust brought him deeper and deeper into her warm and welcoming body.

Once he had sheathed himself fully Daisy wrapped her legs around his waist and gripped his arms at the elbow.

"You are not going to leave me unsatisfied again." She gasped as he thrust home hard.

"No. I am not." Lionel replied, carefully sliding a hand over her mouth. "And you are not going to be heard or alert anyone to what we are doing together."

He watched her eyes light up and felt a squeeze around his shaft. The woman was excited at the idea of being forced to silence? He smiled and moved his head to take one of her breasts into his mouth as he began to move inside her. Slowly building his speed as Daisy moaned against his hand Lionel was soon thundering so forcefully into her willing warmth that he had to hold on to the edge of the table instead of her hip.

"Oh gods." Lionel groaned as Daisy began to buck and writhe, her body tightening and releasing around him in a rapid series of climaxes. "You are a sinful delight, woman."

His own body was nearing the point of explosive release, but he had to keep her quiet until they were both finished, he could not risk a final cry waking the other guests, especially Gerard and Saffir.

When she lifted her hips against him and squeezed his shaft once again it was more than the young knight would resist and he quickly withdrew a brief second before his seed spirted across Daisy's stomach and golden womanly curls.

"I hope that I did not hurt you." He said quietly, after adjusting himself to be decent and using the cloth from another table to clean the mess that they'd made.

"Once you started to pay attention I had a wonderful time. I hope you sleep well, Sir Lionel." Daisy said, laying a kiss on his cheek before heading out towards the kitchen. "Have a safe journey."

"I will." He said, turning to make his way up to his bed. He wanted to tell her that it was not the journey that was the threat but the arrival and what he would find when he got to his childhood home.

Chapter 5

Morning came and Lionel joined Saffir and Gerard for breakfast, not reacting when it was Daisy who was serving their table. The past was the past and he had no intention of giving the girl hope for something that could never be. There was so much more he had to concentrate on. A few days from now they would be arriving at Scotsbane. Gerard and Saffir might stay one night, if he was lucky, then they would be off to get the royal twins which would leave him alone with Fiona and his father.

He was not ready for this, he had no other choice, but he was still not ready.

"Did you sleep alright last night, Lionel?" Gerard asked once Daisy cleared the table and the bills was settled. "I did not hear you come back to our room last night."

"It was, uh, late. I spent some time here by the fire." Lionel said, avoiding the smirk on Daisy's face when he realized that they were sitting at the same table he had ravaged her on only hours before. "I was deep in thought, very deep."

"I see." Saffir said, arching one of his dark eyebrows when he caught a glance that Daisy shot towards the table. "Deep in...thought. Alone?"

"I highly doubt it matters who he was with if anyone. Sir Rule-and-Regulations would hardly know how to have a one-night stand anyway." Gerard said, shoving both Saffir and Lionel towards the door with a shake of his head. "There is no time for anything more than thoughts. There are people waiting, and while the twins might be patient, death is not. Lionel must get home before that spectre comes calling."

"Do not remind me of that, please." Lionel said to Gerard. "I'm not so proper as you assume, old man. I simply have the manners to never speak of my liaisons."

He mounted his horse and cast a glance over his shoulder. "Unless the two of you have farewells of your own to say then let us depart. I would like to be north of the capitol before nightfall."

"Lead the way then, lover-boy." Saffir teased. "I would not want to upset your fire light plans."

"You are an ass Saffir." Lionel said, nudging his heels in and heading north towards Camelot leaving the inn and its inhabitants behind with his friends following after him.

Saffir might be trying to make him laugh, but it was not working. They would understand soon enough. When they met his father both of them might stop. They did not know what he did, that it as likely that he would not be returning with them to Redbourne, now or ever. There was no other heir than himself. Sir Alex would never allow Fiona to inherit the property, even if she knew it better than anyone else every could.

He managed to ignore the teasing for a few hours. Once they understood that he was not going to give them the reaction that they wanted and that they would not be able to improve his mood Saffir and Gerard left Lionel alone with his thoughts. He wondered if, while his father had been searching for a husband for Fiona, Sir Alex had been looking for some woman that was socially suitable to be Lionel's wife? Had Daisy been the last woman he would enjoy as a single man?

"Lionel? Lionel!" Gerard's voice pulled him out of his thoughts. "Are you sure that you do not want to stop in Camelot? Take the chance to pay respects to the king? It might give you some clout to use to impress your father."

"Nothing I do or say short of arriving as a newly crowned king would impress my father and even then, he would condemn me for not doing it sooner or allowing him to plan my coronation." Lionel said with a shrug. "That is why it is useless to go to Camelot unless there is need to deliver a missive from Liam."

"I have no papers from Liam." Gerard sounded slightly disappointed. Things had been a bit strained between the two friends since Liam had married Caelia.

They had been different between Lionel and Gerard as well since he had caught the blacksmith in the arms of the Prince of Gore on a staircase in Camelot the night that Liam and Caelia got married. It was not against the old religion for men, or women to be lovers but the new church deemed that it was an unholy act and a great "sin". He thought it was ridiculous to ban love but was still unsure how he felt about Liam and Gerard's incredibly close friendship and even less sure how he felt about Gerard and the Prince. That was a commoner and a Royal, almost impossible to maintain or get approval for. Would they want to marry? Each other? Or was this simply no more than lust?

"Then let us avoid the city and all within it that would delay our arrival and thus delay our departure as well." Lionel said, riding past the turn towards the city. "I cannot say often enough how much I do not want to be at my father's house."

"Is it not your house, since the old man is dying?" Saffir asked, dodging the dark look from Gerard. "What? That is why he is returning, because his father is dying. It is not rude to state the truth."

"There is such a thing as tact and you seem to be lacking in it entirely, Saffir." Gerard said, rolling his eyes. "That fact is what makes timing this journey harder to arrange. We do not know how long Lionel is going to need at Scotsbane, and the twins are eager to leave Gore and journey south to Redbourne. Either Lionel will be alone with his sister after the passing or we will bring the twins to Scotsbane and join him there."

"I have no desire to stay longer than needed, Gerard." Lionel said. "Bring Elin and Banning at their leisure, we will leave when you arrive. I do not need to be there for the funeral his friends in the new religion will give him. My farewell will be brief. I will gather my sister and whatever she needs and then we will return to Redbourne with the rest of you."

"You may find that harder than you think, Sir Lionel." A familiar voice said from the side of the road as a golden-haired knight stepped out of the forest. "It would have been better if you had stopped in to see the king. There are things you need to know."

"Lancelot." Gerard growled. "Still a nosy bastard sticking yourself where you do not belong?"

"Gerard, still a surly beast of a man I see. How very charming." Lancelot said stepping up to Lionel's horse after giving Saffir a nod.

"Always a pleasure to see you, Sir Lancelot. What do you mean there are things that I need to know? What is going on up North?" Lionel said, ignoring Gerard's tension and glare at the King's right-hand man.

"That new religion, priests and nuns and such, are taking over the entire country. They are starting with the older estates, like Scotsbane. The latest letter that Arthur received said that, if you do as expected and leave, they will turn the entire place, lands and buildings, into what they call a monastery."

"What is a monastery?" Saffir asked with a tilt of his head. "Is that some kind farm?"

"A farm of people. That is where they house their monks and nuns, where they brainwash people to following their commandments." Lancelot scoffed. "A perfect waste of lives and a way for them to make money."

"Does Arthur want me to stay at Scotsbane? Leave Redbourne and the others?" Lionel asked, frowning deeply at the thought. As much as they were awkward together, a strange little group, they had become a family and that meant more to him than a title and land. Even if it was at the request of the king he was not willing to walk away from the people who mattered most to him.

"The letters from your father state that it is your duty to do so. The king strongly encourages you consider that." Lancelot said.

"I have no intention of staying there. Whatever his majesty wants done with the property can be done, but I will not be the one to do it." Lionel said firmly.

"Who is going to be left to do it then boy?" Lancelot said, shaking his head and glancing at Gerard. "Has Liam not taught them about taking responsibility for their families? Some things come before adventure."

"I am hardly a boy anymore, Sir." Lionel said, bringing a mocking grin from the older knight. "I will leave no one behind that does not wish for it. Estate managers have surely been doing the majority of the work since my father's decline. If the man is responsible enough then I shall have him continue and make the journey to inspect the property quarterly."

He knew that more than half of the knights in Camelot, especially the senior ones, did the same thing with their estates. They often left wives and children behind so that they could enjoy the pleasures of the capital without the encumbrance tied to being a family man.

"You think that will keep this new church from claiming the property? The lands? The people? Your own sister could be coerced into joining them, you know that?" Lancelot said, the grin disappearing.

"I doubt that my sister would join such a thing, willingly." Lionel said, trying to hide the realization that a lot had likely changed for her as well, in the years he had been gone. Was she still stubborn with a touch of wildness or had their father forced her to submit to his will at last? "Even if she did, the estate would only fall to her upon my demise. Do you think that these new priests would commit murder simply to take control of some land?"

He was beginning to worry that his father would have things in place when he got there so that he could force an impossible ultimatum on his son. Stay home or be the cause of the suffering of everyone he loved.

"I think they have already done so. Gerard did not tell you?" Lancelot looked at the blacksmith. "The steward of his own home died under mysterious circumstances before being bought by the church earlier this month. As for your sister, if she is not to be a nun then she might well wish that she were. The men that have declared to be in talks with your father for her hand are not ones that I would wish upon an enemy, let alone a beloved sister."

"What? Does Liam know this Gerard Why did you stay? I thought you had family there still? Do they work for this church or were they turned out?" Saffir joined the conversation to ask.

"Liam does not know. He will when we return with the royal twins. They are going to help me find a way to save the place." Gerard growled, pulling his horse's head free from Lancelot's grip. "We should ride if we do not want to have to do the same for Scotsbane, unless you have changed your mind and wish to stop in Camelot?"

"Give our respects to the king, Sir." Lionel said, trying to stay civil and as calm as he could while facing the possibility of what his father might be up to and what he might be facing after the old bastard died. "We ride for Scotsbane with haste."

When the senior man nodded and stepped back from the horses, Lionel dug in his heels and took off up the road.

"We will make it in time, Lionel." Gerard said, keeping pace with him while Saffir brought up the rear. "Lancelot enjoys playing with the minds of others while he tugs, relentlessly, on their heartstrings. He always has and always will."

Chapter 6

For the rest of the day Lionel puzzled over Gerard's words regarding Lancelot. He had been considered to be the champion of Briton for more than fifteen years and was the closest friend to the king. Even Liam had a grudging respect for the man, but it felt as though Gerard was ready to cross steel with him at the drop of a hat.

What had caused that kind of anger to linger for all the years that the knights had known each other? Why did Gerard carry such a vehement grudge?

It was impossible to ask him. Though there was little else to do but talk as they rode neither Saffir nor Lionel dared to bring it up. They spoke on every subject under the sun except the one that they wanted to speak of most. Even during the nights by the fireside, there was a definite standoffish air around Gerard's shoulders that made it uncomfortable to speak of much besides Lionel's childhood home.

As they drew nearer to the property it seemed as though the memories of the good times grew stronger and the darker, traumatic ones faded with the comparison. With Saffir's questions, as well a few more technical ones from Gerard, Lionel found himself talking more about the adventures that he had enjoyed with the other children. Lessons learned from the farmers and other tradesmen were easier to recall when he was sharing the information with his friends.

Lionel wished that they could stay at Scotsbane with him to see this finished, but that was not the purpose of their attendance. He would have to do this on his own, proving to his father and himself that he was more than the bookish boy he had been when he left. Any other father could be counted on to be impressed when his only son became a knight, an expert swordsman, and an awarded archer, but not Sir Alex. His letters over the years indicated that none of these accomplishments meant anything to him. He simply wanted his son to be married, producing children and at Scotsbane where he could be controlled, molded into an exact replica of his father, and do what was expected when it was expected.

Lionel had no desire to be a part of any of that.

"Is that Scotsbane over there?" Saffir asked, pulling Lionel from his thoughts.

He was pointing towards the dark, stone house at the crest of a gentle hill overlooking the farmland around them. Lionel noticed that the people working in the fields had begun to gather. They were pointing and muttering amongst themselves, obviously trying to discern who the trio of knights were. Lionel wondered if his father had alerted the tenants that he was returning home or if this was a surprise for them as well.

"Yes it is." He replied to Saffir. "It looks as though my father has lit the fires of welcome for us too."

The windows of the main floor were all lit brightly, which told Lionel that there would be a dinner planned to show Gerard and Saffir the wealth and privilege that their friend was turning down. The games of guilt started long before the discussions began and would last long after the man left this world.

"Are you ready for this Lionel?" Gerard asked, pausing his horse next to him. "If you are not, we can go to the inn instead. Have a pint before facing the old boar?"

"No." Lionel shook his head and nudged his horse forwards again. "I might as well face him now. Get it over with."

They started down the road towards the house, watching as a young boy took off running from the field. Undoubtedly, he was going to tell the lord of the manner that the prodigal son was approaching so that the pageantry could begin.

"Besides, if I am going to have a drink I will need it later tonight after talking with my father more than I do now."

"Then let's hope he keeps his cellars well stocked." Saffir said, laughing as they rode up to the house where footmen were waiting for them.

"That you can always be assured of." Lionel said dismounting and handing over the reins before addressing the man at the door. "I assume that my father is expecting me?"

"Yes, master Lionel. I believe he is in the hall with the lady Fiona awaiting your arrival for the meal." He said with a bored tone.

"That is Sir Lionel to you and all here." Gerard interjected roughly. "The man stands a knight of Arthur's court and should be treated with the respect due his position."

"The man stood a boy the last time he darkened these halls, Sir." The Servant stated flatly. "It might take some adjusting for the staff to see him as more than such."

"They had better adjust fast then." Saffir said with a smirk. "If it is true that Sir Alex is about to depart this world who do you think is going to be in charge around here?"

"Who indeed, Sir." The servant said, opening the door to the dining hall.

Lionel looked down the length of the table where he had eaten daily as a child and met the cold, dark eyes of his father.

A shiver ran down his spine and into his gut.

Even weakened and dying the old monster had a glare that could stop the blood in Lionel's veins.

It was like staring down the blade of an executioner's sword and he froze for a moment.

"Lionel? Is it really you brother?"

Fiona's voice cut the tension and brought a smile to Lionel's face. He shook off the fears from his childhood and remembered that he was not a scared little boy any longer. Knights fought monsters and did not cower from them. Neither would he.

"Yes, little sister. I am all grown up now, as are you." He opened his arms for her as she rushed from their father's side to throw her arms around his neck.

The impact of her embrace spun him in a circle. Over the top of her head he saw a genuine smile on Gerard's face and shock at his show of affection on Saffir's. This was a side of him that they had never seen and the man they knew was one that his sweet sister would not recognize as her beloved brother.

"You certainly are. Look at you." Fiona smiled up at him.

Taking his hand, she pulled him away from the other knights and towards the other end of the table.

"You and I are not the only ones who have grown up." She said enthusiastically. "Surely you remember Moira and Lilith from our childhood?"

"Ladies. It is good to see you again." Lionel managed to choke when both women turned to flash smiles at him that dazzled like the gems in the crown of Camelot. These were not the same gangly, awkwardly lovely girls they had been when he and Moira had laid together for his first time as a man. Moira was willow thin with pale, creamy skin, and jet-black hair. Her dark brown eyes sparked with recognition and Lionel was sure that she remembered their time together as clearly as he did. Lilith had more curve to her form than he remembered, in every area a man could desire. Her hair was a glossy brown that shone in the candlelight, but it was her hazel eyes sparking with agitation that caught his attention.

"Hello Lilith, Moira, you have both, um, grown up." He said with a smile when she caught him staring.

"Hello, Sir Lionel. You are as stellar a conversationalist as ever I see." Was Lilith's clipped response.

Lionel nodded with a blush rising on his cheeks. She had always been able to embarrass him with her cleverness and intense stare. It did not seem to have changed, though he had hoped she might see something more than the boy he used to be.

"You are as poorly mannered too." Sir Alex said, glaring at his son from his chair. "I would have thought that, as a knight, you would have learned some of that courtly behavior. You ought to know that propriety states that I should have been addressed first. As your father and as a knight of the realm I should have been the first."

It did not matter that he was right, Lionel wanted to object, to argue, that one had to prove themselves worthy of any honor. That was what Alex had beaten into him every day, every time he had tried to stand up for himself, or someone else. His father had made sure that Lionel knew that he was less of a man than his father was, that he was a disappointment. Those beatings were what had driven him to be the best, to work the hardest of all the young knights in Camelot.

Lionel had been the best swordsman and the most loyal man of all those that had left Camelot with Liam when he was banished to Redbourne. There was never a moment that he regretted it either. Departing court and the finery to live at the great hall that was rough in comparison to the grand dining hall with the king was easy when he knew that he was doing the right thing.

"You have my apologies father. I wish that I could say I hope you are feeling well." Lionel said, forcing himself to stay calm and polite. The mere sight of his father, however feeble he looked, set him on edge and sharpened his tongue so strongly that it took great strength of will, to force himself to be polite.

"Of course, I do not feel well. I am dying Lionel. In case you forgot that. Your sister and Moira do their best to make sure that I am as comfortable as possible." Sir Alex said with a growl.

"Lilith helps too father." Fiona said. She frowned at their father but when she turned to face Lionel she was smiling again. "Truly brother, I do not know how we would be able to manage around here without them both. I do not know how I will manage without them should I leave here either."

"Well, we will figure something out when the time comes. Nothing to worry about until then." Lionel said, taking the seat left empty on his father's right side. "This is Sir Gerard, Sir Liam's friend and right-hand man. Also, Saffir who was in my class of squires in Camelot years ago and joined the lot of us at Redbourne."

"I would say that you are Liam's right hand, Lionel, and I his left." Gerard said, taking a seat next to Lionel.

"They say that the left hand is the one knights of Camelot used to wipe their asses." Sir Alex said.

"The do say that." Gerard replied, with a sly smile. "They use it more often to hold a shield though, at least more often than those who set swords aside for wine glasses years ago."

Saffir tried to hide his chuckle in his hand and Lionel choked on his own wine while Sir Alex sputtered with rage.

"You are impertinent, Sir. I expected better from a senior knight claiming to be an intimate of Sir Liam, especially when he is so freshly welcomed back to the court of the king. You would not wish for your behaviors to reflect poorly upon him."

"Father, it was a joke." Lionel tried to calm him while watching Fiona struggle to keep a straight face. The feeling, the fear of his father's reaction, took him right back to his childhood and the need to protect everyone around him, especially his sister.

The man could be a monster and the words he was capable of lashing out could leave scars worse that the whip of a squire-master or that crop that Saffir used on himself when he considered himself to have sinned greatly before the gods.

"Well, lads, welcome to Scotsbane. Where my father's legendary jokes often look like threats to the realm and the king."

Chapter 7

Lilith sat stunned at the table as the others chattered around her. The knights mildly flirtatious efforts with the women and bantering with each other with the familiarity of brothers were oddly familial. She could hardly help but to smile at the stories that Saffir and Gerard shared about Lionel after Fiona begged them for tales about her brother. She could not remember the last time this house had seemed so cheerful, even if was a temporary thing.

Fiona was smiling brighter now than she had for weeks, staring at her brother as though he was Lancelot or King Arthur. Lilith noticed Moira batting her lashes, trying to get the attention of the blacksmith, Gerard.

The man seemed to be ignoring her advances, even though Lilith was certain that the man was unmarried. It must be driving Moira mad, no one ignored her, ever. That fact in itself was enough to make Lilith want to laugh, but it would be considered rude. She would probably have to explain herself to Sir Alex if she did that. He was not one to enjoy laughter, even that of Elaine when she was playing. Lilith laughing at the indignation of the woman next to her when she was not flirted with would likely be met with even less tolerance. No matter how annoying Moira could be it would be considered rude by the head of the house.

"Lilith? Lilith what are you daydreaming of?" Moira asked, simultaneously interrupting her thoughts, and proving her point.

"Just planning out the day tomorrow. I am sure that Sir Lionel..."

"Just Lionel please, Lilith." The distractingly handsome man corrected her.

"Thank you, Lionel. I am sure that Lionel is going to want a tour of the grounds and the estate tomorrow. I was merely doing a mental review of what rooms still need to be prepared for a proper viewing. I am certain that you will want to ensure that the staff are turned out and on their best behavior, since we must all do out part to impress the next lord of the manor."

"I certainly intend to do everything that I can to impress m'lord Lionel." Moira said with a smile as she leaned forward across the table.

Lilith rolled her eyes and shared a glance with Fiona. The woman was grotesquely obvious and while Gerard and Lionel seemed to be completely immune to her, Saffir was certainly mesmerized. Too bad he would find himself at the bottom of her effort list unless further conversation revealed the man to somehow outclass the other two.

"I am not a member of the house of Lords, Moira. Even my father has not been awarded such an honor, though perhaps someday I will be able to advance our family name in such a way."

"I doubt that entirely." Sir Alex joined the dialogue. "How in heavens could you surpass my accomplishments in the eyes of the king and court? Got another dishonored knight you can run after, claiming loyalty to a dishonest man?"

"Sir Liam has been found innocent of those accusations and been restored to the favor of the King." Gerard growled, slamming his cup down to the tabletop. "If you bothered to show up at court you would know better than to speak such things."

"It is rather hard for a dying man to travel, Sir Gerard. I can hardly be expected to waste my precious time left on this earth ensuring that every criminal in Camelot stays where they belong."

Lilith thought that the blacksmith was going to throw his glass and attack Sir Alex physically, thus ending the wait for his demise. Saffir and Lionel both must have seen what she saw because Saffir put his hand on the older man's forearm and Lionel stood up to face his father.

"You know Liam better than that, father, or used to. Just because he never liked you or agreed with your policies does not make him a criminal." Lionel said with a strain in his voice that Lilith recognized from their childhood. Whenever he had to stand up to his father for Fiona's sake, or at times, his own, his voice had taken that same tone. It usually led to her finding him in the barns later, seeking the calming comfort of the animals.

Once she had found him sitting in the straw with the head of a young calf in his lap. The little one was nearly asleep, and Lionel was talking to it so sweetly with a tone so gentle Lilith had stopped to listen. She still remembered the agony in his voice as he told the sleeping calf about the heartbreak of never being good enough for his father, how he knew that he would never meet his standards and his deep desire to leave Scotsbane for Camelot so that he had a chance at making a name for himself instead.

It had been heartbreaking to hear the young man who wanted nothing more than to please the only parent he had left. Instead he was constantly being torn down. Lilith had wanted to help him see that he was worth so much more than his father would let him believe. She had wanted to go to him and hold him tight until he no longer hurt. She did not get the chance though.

Before Lilith took the chance to let Lionel know that she was there a guardsman from the house came to summon him back to the house at the command of his father.

The resignation on his face as he got to his feet and left the comfort of the barn and animal still stuck in Lilith's mind to that day. She wondered if he remembered that day as well?

"I do not care what he managed to convince Arthur to say." Sir Alex countered his son.

"You mean King Arthur, Sir Alex. There is no allowance for such informality despite our distance from the capitol." Gerard said. The hard edge to his voice was unmistakable and Lilith decided that it was a good idea to take the initiative to end the meal right there.

"Sir Gerard, Lionel, Sir Saffir. Perhaps now would be a good time to show you to your rooms?" She offered. Speaking loudly to ensure that each man at the table remember that there were ladies present before tempers were lost entirely. "If you will come with me I would be happy to escort you as I am certain you must be tired from the day and your time on the road. Lady Moira can attend to Sir Alex, so you need not trouble yourselves."

"Thank you, Lilith. I think that would be better for everyone." Lionel said, getting up from the table and giving his father a slight bow. "I will speak with you more in the morning, father. Good rest to you Fiona, you as well Moira."

Lilith kept her eyes down and avoided smiling while escorting the knights from the room under the matching glares of Sir Alex and Moira. She might not be able to save Lionel from his father completely, but she managed to save him tonight and that was enough for now. The other two knights were on their own. She did not know them well enough to be willing to risk the anger of Sir Alex, even if it would not last much longer. She should feel bad that the man was dying and would not be missed by anyone except Fiona, but she did not. He was too much of a beast for her to have any compassion left for him.

"This room is for you Sir Saffir and this one, across the hall, is for you Sir Gerard." She said with a polite smile as she opened the doors.

"Thank you, Lilith." Gerard said, stepping inside. "I hope that it locks from the inside. I would hate to wake up with Moira standing over me, or worse."

Lilith giggled while pretending to look shocked.

"Sir Gerard, I assure you that we do not encourage such behavior in this house. Despite her somewhat forward nature Moira is a lady and will behave as one if she wants to keep her position."

"Thank you Lilith." Gerard said with a devilish grin that she could not deny sent a thrill through her. "I shall sleep well knowing that my virtue is safe within your walls."

"I am glad that I could ease your troubled mind Sir Gerard." Lilith replied with a smile. It felt like the teasing between friends that she used to have with Lionel. Even though she did not know this man or, truthfully, the one that she used to know well enough to tease like that, this felt good, comfortable.

"I think I will leave my door unlatched." Saffir said. "In case the poor woman needs consoling from Ger's rejection."

"I hope, for your sake, that you do not end up regretting that choice, Sir Saffir."

Lilith shook her head and gestured to Lionel.

"I'll take you to your room so you can get some rest before dealing with your father, Lionel. I know it is not easy, any of this, but you do not have to do it all alone." She said once they were away from the others. "Fiona manages him quite well and Moira does help, in her way. Despite the flirting tonight she is a very capable nurse. Somehow they manage to get along alright."

"What about you? How do you get along? Do you spend more time with my sister or does Moira?" Lionel asked, increasing his pace to walk beside her.

She wondered if he noticed that the back of his hand had brushed across hers. It had felt like a bolt of lightening, but perhaps that was simply because it had been years since she had experienced the touch of a man in such a potentially intimate setting. In the years before he had left, it would not have been possible to think that Lionel might use such a moment to try and flirt his way into a kiss. If he had the nerve to try it that is. He had always been so shy when they were alone together like this.

Now he seemed a man full of outside knowledge and, perhaps, a little more confidence in himself than before. It was an appealing thought, no matter how impossible it was. He was the new lord of Scotsbane, or would be, as well as Fiona's brother. They had been friends once, long ago, but now she was the servant and he was her master.

"I was employed to serve your sister, though I do my best to help everywhere I can around here when I can." She said, guiding him down the hallway towards his room.

"When you can? Does Fiona keep you horribly busy?" Lionel asked, stopping in front of the elaborately carved door of his bedroom. "I always thought her to be rather independent."

"She still is, which is what makes this position perfect for me." Lilith said, letting the door swing open for him. "I hope everything is satisfactory. I prepared it myself."

"I am afraid that I still do not understand what..."

He was cut off by the one person who could answer every question he had and the one that she had hoped he would not meet by surprise.

"Mama! Mama! I could not find you. I had a bad dream." Elaine, in her little white nightdress, clutching her blanket was running down the hall with bare feet. "I called and I called, but you did not hear me. Who is that?"

Elaine had wrapped her arms around Lilith's legs and was staring at Lionel from behind her.

"Mama? Who is this little kitten?" Lionel said, crouching down to meet her eyes. "My name is Lionel. I grew up here, a long time ago. I used to have bad dreams too."

"You did? You are so big though. What were you afraid of?" Elain asked, stepping out from behind Lilith.

"Elaine, dear, let Mama take you back to bed and you can ask Sir Alex's son your questions another time. He is just as tired as you are."

"Alright Mama. Goodnight Lionel, Sir." She said with a yawn before turning back in the direction she came.

"Sleep well, Elaine." Lionel said with a smile that warmed Lilith's heart. It was a tender, smile, with a warmth he certainly did not learn from his father. "Oh, and I used to be afraid of mice. That is why I have a cat at home, so that I am not afraid anymore."

Elaine giggled and started down the hall, with a few glances over her shoulder towards the knight and her mother.

"I will be right there, sweetheart." Lilith said with a nod.

"You have a daughter Lilith? You did not say you were married? Where is her father?"

His curiosity was so genuine, and he seemed so interested in the answers. She hated to have to tell the truth, but she learned a long time ago that the truth was the best weapon against the judgments of others. No one could hurt her with what they thought of her if she did not care.

"I am not married, Lionel. Elaine's father left before she was born and I came to work here, for your sister, just afterwards. I do not hide it, nor am I ashamed that I believed him when he said he loved me and wanted to marry me. His lies and desertion make him a coward and my devotion to my daughter makes me..."

"Incredibly strong and brave." Lionel finished for her. "I will not keep you from her tonight, but I would like to discuss the situation more in the coming days as it pertains to the estate. Good night."

Chapter 8

Lilith was a mother, an unwed mother, and she worked for his father. Either his father had changed more than Lionel ever thought possible or this was the work of Fiona. Moira would not have helped to bring this about, she was too set on pleasing his father, but his little sister could be amazingly compassionate and fantastically stubborn if she set her mind to it.

He was still having a hard time believing that Lilith was a mother.

What fool of a man had done that to her? Not the bedding part, it was easy to see why any and every man in the area would have been sniffing after her like a hound at the scent. Why would a man leave a woman like that, unmarried. She was as incredible now as she had been when they were children together, perhaps more so. She was independent and intimidating, but he suspected that there was a softness there too, behind the armour she put up around her heart.

He locked the door behind himself, Lilith was right about Moira sneaking into bedrooms, and looked around the same room he had as a young man. It was all so familiar and yet it felt like a totally different life.

Sitting on the stool that was still just beside the door, Lionel took off his boots and set them on the shelf that he had made as a boy. He hated tracking dirt into his room because he loved to walk barefoot as much as possible. The floorboards were smooth, worn down by years of a nervous boy's pacing and they still felt soothing beneath the feet of a grown man come home.

The rest of the room was just as familiar. Dark stained wood everywhere, from the spiraling columns of his four-post bed to the intricately carved wardrobe door as well as the heavy, ornate desk that was positioned to look out the window down into the training field. He could still see the grooves on the floor where he had pushed and dragged it from its original position facing the wall.

He had argued with his father about the placement and the old man had finally told him that if he could move it himself then he would not have it moved back. It had taken Lionel hours and strained muscles, plus the gouges on the floor to get it where he wanted it to be, but it was his first victory over his father. Thus, it was his favorite piece of furniture in the room.

As much as good manners said that he should unpack his bag, hang things in the wardrobe and tuck away in drawers, he was looking forward to laying in his old bed too much to do any unpacking tonight. He set the bag on the chair and started to undress in the light of the candles. The distraction of Lilith being a mother was still weighing on Lionel's mind, so he did not hear the sound of the servant door opening or hear the footsteps coming across floor. When Moira put her hands on his shoulders he spun on his heel and knocked her to her back on the bed.

"Welcome home, lover." She smiled up at him. "I guess asking if you want to pick up where we left off is a little irrelevant."

"It is unnecessary, because it is not happening, Moira." Lionel grunted, crossing his arms across his chest, and leaning against one of the pillars. "What are you doing here?"

"I thought that was obvious. I am here to see you. To see you taken care of. You must have a few things you need dealt with after such a long ride."

She ran her hands up his thighs to loop her fingers at the top of his breeches. Staring up at his bare chest Lionel could tell that she was salivating at the idea of a much more physical reunion. Too bad he did not share the interest, even though she was right about needs and wants after a long ride. He was not sure that she wanted anything more than another chance to get herself attached to the heir of the house, but he was too tired for games tonight.

"Moira. I just got home, and I do not particularly want to be here. You know how badly I wanted to get away. On top of that, my father is dying and determined to make me miserable before he goes. I do not have the patience for playing games."

He took hold of her wrists and detached them from his pants.

"I am going to bed, alone. Saffir might enjoy getting to know you better if you are looking for a fun evening." Lionel said, trying to sound bored instead of annoyed.

"You would just pawn me off on your friend? What kind of woman do you think I am?" She pouted, turning her hands to take hold of his. "Do you not like me anymore? Or do you have a lady waiting for you at Redbourne?"

"No. There is no one and that is just as I would have it." He said with a frown, detangling their hands. "Until I have things more settled in my life and know what I want to do with it I am no going to involve another person in it, no matter what I feel for them."

She smiled and got to her feet.

"You admit you still have feelings for me? Perhaps, while you are home, I will be able to convince the big brooding knight of Camelot to let someone in."

She sauntered to the door, making sure that the sway of her hips was as eye catching as possible.

"Goodnight Moira. Pleasant dreams." He said, unlocking and opening the door. "Try to leave Saffir alive at least."

Lionel shook his head when she laughed, some people did not change, but the smile on his lips fell when he saw Lilith standing in the hallway, witnessing the other woman leave his room.

Shit.

He found himself worrying that she would think that Moira had accomplished what she had set out to do. Somehow that false impression mattered more to him than he anticipated. He did not want Lilith to think that he was starting something with Moira.

"Lilith? I...what are you doing here? It is not what you think." He stammered awkwardly.

"Of course not, Sir Lionel." She said, her voice tight. "Goodnight, Sir."

She turned and rushed down the hallway, leaving Lionel flustered, annoyed and even more tired than he had been five minutes ago.

"Shit." He muttered to himself then stepped back into his room and locked the door again. "That was a disaster."

He shucked off his pants and sat on the edge of his bed. Falling backwards across the mattress Lionel groaned. He had been home less than four hours and he had already irritated his father, disappointed both the women from his childhood and with his luck the first person he spoke to in the morning would be his sister and he would do something to upset her too. How could his luck be so rotten that Lilith would see him escorting Moira out of his room, right after she had warned them all about her forward manners.

She obviously thought that Moira had done what she had intended. What Lionel could not wrap his mind around was that it mattered to Lilith. She was bothered by the idea that he might have been intimate with Moira. She had not flirted with him or given him any idea that she was interested in him, so why was she upset?

If they had ever been together he would have been worried that the child was his, but the closest they had ever come was a few awkward kisses years before he had left Scotsbane the first time. It had to be something else.

Women were confusing creatures.

He got beneath the covers and punched the pillow to fluff it up as he crashed his head onto it. What should have been a good sleep, full of rest, was now full of questions instead. He tossed and turned, changing position over a dozen times before he finally fisted his cock in frustration. Stroking away the questions and doubts, the mind games, and little tricks that he had played on him by women of the court of Camelot over the years before going to Redbourne with Liam. The games of flirtation had been different, but the end game had been the same.

They all wanted to get married, to bind themselves to a man with a future beyond what they could see for themselves. None of them actually cared who he was or wanted to get to know him, they just wanted a new life and saw him as the way to get to get it. Just once he wanted the woman he was with to want to be with him, not with his title or his future potential. He wanted someone who wanted him for his personality, who actually cared about him and what he wanted.

If his father had his way he would be married off to some heiress or the daughter of one of his friends so that it was a marriage of proper standing at court. Love mattered less to his father than keeping up the proper appearances. It was horrible enough for Lionel, to be paired off to some girl who only needed to be of childbearing age and from a proper family to be deemed suitable, but Fiona could be married off to any of his father's friends that could still stand up to say the vows and had the virility to bed her.

The thought turned his stomach. Fiona was sweet, kind, and innocent as well as beautiful. She certainly did not deserve to have that taken away by some disgusting old man that wanted her simply because she was pretty and could bear him more children than he already had. The girl deserved more than a knight. She should be with a king, one that would treat her as she deserved and make sure that she was never treated badly again. He would settle for a prince, as long as he was from a southern kingdom that would keep her closer to him at Redbourne.

Lionel was still determined that he would not be staying in the north. His work with Liam was not nearly done and he truly hated it here despite the familiarity. He had to find someone that he could trust to run the estate after his father passed, someone that cared about this place and, most importantly, cared about the people who lived on the land. No matter what relationship he had with his father he had to admit that the man had managed Scotsbane and the people who depended on it better than anyone else he had ever seen. Once he found someone who could do that then he could leave and only come back when it was absolutely needed.

If Fiona married then her children could be the heirs to this place, and he could be free of it forever. He did not even need to take a wife if he managed to get her happily married.

He rolled over with a groan. That was how easy it was to become a man like his father that was controlling of everything and everyone around him. It started with doing things for the good of others, but there was no telling how quickly it could, and would, turn into doing things the way that he wanted under the pretence that it was better for everyone if things went his way.

Lionel wondered if that was how his father had begun when he had taken over here? Had the angry, demanding, demeaning, man once thought that he was doing what was best for everyone he cared about by taking away their choice? Had it all been his way of trying to protect them? How long had it taken for reason and respect to turn to madness and manipulations?

"Will that be me, in the end? Will I be like him?" He asked the dark before rolling over to stare out the window while he waited for sleep to take him. "Or will I break free of him at last?"

Chapter 9

Lilith was as flustered in the morning as she had been the evening before when she had found Moira exiting Lionel's room. While the other woman had revealed years ago that they had shared their first intimacies with each other Lilith did not think that there had been any lingering attachment between them. Moira certainly had not behaved like a woman missing a man that she cared for and, though she was enthusiastic when the letter came that Lionel was returning to Scotsbane, she certainly had not expressed her affection.

Perhaps she had been wrong though? Perhaps her friend was good at hiding such things and had merely been waiting for the man to appear.

As she prepared the breakfast trays for Lionel, Elaine, and Sir Alex, getting them ready to be taken upstairs by the maids to be served in bed, Lilith had to stop and force herself to consider what she was truly feeling.

Jealous.

She was jealous at the thought that Moira had been in Lionel's bed last night.

For years in their youth Lilith had thought that she might have had a chance at romance with Lionel. So many of their friends and classmates from the monk's school had eventually coupled up and gotten married for love or were betrothed. There were even a few that had been forced to marry due to scandal, as she had almost been forced when she became pregnant with Elaine.

If her lover had not left in order to escape such a fate she likely would have been enslaved in a marriage to a man that did not love her, the mother of as many children as he decided to force upon her between the affairs he would no doubt have. He had wanted marriage and a family even less than she had at that time. Her father had been extremely displeased when she told him that she would not willingly marry anyone, but when there was no one that could be forced or bribed into marrying her he came to accept her condition.

Sadly, he died only a few months after Elaine was born and never got to fully enjoy being a grandfather.

The priests had taken her father's property, since there was no male heir, and had tried to force her into the cloister of nuns. Lilith had refused them adamantly. They seemed greedy and lecherous, the very opposite of everything they preached in their sermons. Lilith was not about to trust them with her safety and well-being and certainly not that of her daughter. She thought that she would have to find a way to leave the town and try to start over somewhere new when Fiona came to her aid.

The friendship with Lionel's sister had been as organic as the one with the man himself and Lilith was glad to have kept in touch. The younger girl's plan to have Lilith fully integrated into the household and well liked by Sir Alex before he realized that she had a daughter out of wedlock went better than they could have hoped. The old knight had adored Lilith, doting on her. He smiled and even flirted a little bit. Those few months had been such a happy time for the entire household. Fiona had once even teased that she thought her father would propose marriage. Then, thanks to Moira, Sir Alex found out about Elaine.

His reaction was the opposite of what Lionel's had been. The elder knight had raged and swore. Cursing Lilith for what he saw as a deception. He accused her of lying and sneaking Elaine onto the property. Stealing food, clothing, and extra supplies in general, as well as stealing the time of other staff members to help hide the child and take care of her. He had wanted to throw them both out until Fiona intervened. She begged her father to let them stay and reminded him of how much he enjoyed Lilith's company. He was still determined to have her removed from his household.

Lilith and Fiona were both out of ideas on how to convince Sir Alex to let her stay. The only thing they had not tried was a physical seduction and neither girl could stomach that idea. In the end Elaine was the one that solved the problem for them.

The child took advantage of Lilith and Fiona being distracted as they tried to sort out their options and snuck down to the office where Sir Alex had been sitting at his desk, sifting through papers. The little girl had found a plate of sweet pastries and carefully carried it all the way from the kitchen and to the side of the desk.

"Sir Alex?" She said, holding up the plate. "I can help with little things if you let me stay with mama. I promise to be very good and earn my suppers."

That was when Lilith had found them. She could hardly believe the soft look on the knight's face as he considered the offer from the toddler.

"I am so sorry, Sir Alex. She must have heard me talking about what has been going on and thought that this would help to change your mind. I apologize for the bother."

At first he did not say a word, he simply stared down into Elaine's sweet, soft, grey eyes. It looked as though he was studying her very soul. There was an emotion on Sir Alex' face that Lilith did not recognize, a softening of the stony demeanor brought on by the innocent offer of her child. Perhaps there was something more to the old man than she ever suspected. He was capable of love despite his brusque demeanor and it touched Lilith deeply.

"Come, Elaine, we must not bother Sir Alex. He is a busy man with many people relying on him." Lilith said, holding out her hand to beckon her daughter to her side.

"There is no bother." Sir Alex said, coming back to himself and accepting the plate from the outstretched hands. "Take the child back to your rooms and see her settled before the evening meal."

Lilith hardly dared to believe his words. She wanted to ask him to clarify, to confirm that the rooms he had demanded she vacate as soon as possible were hers once again.

"Of course, I will, Sir Alex. She had been upset these past days to see our belongings packed up to leave and has not wanted to stay but I will make sure that she does so tonight."

"Good." He said gruffly then turned his head to look at Elaine once more. He shocked Lilith even further when he held out a baked treat to the little girl. "Well then unpack the damned things and stop upsetting her. It is not good for children to live a life of such uncertainty."

"Yes sir, thank you sir." Lilith bowed her head and did her best to contain her grateful smile so that she did not annoy the man with a show of affection. "I will return things to normal as quickly as possible."

"Just so." Sir Alex said, a small smile teasing his lips when Elaine beamed over her first bite of the sweet.

"Though I will take the girl up on her request for employment. She will take my walks with me, in the gardens, every day after the noon meal. That way I can ensure that she is being brought up correctly and will not turn out to be some wild vagabond with no concept of propriety. How does that sound, little duck?" He asked the child, tapping her nose with the fluffy end of his quill pen. "Keep me company and learn a little?"

"Yes, Sir Alex. Thank you, sir, for the yummy. I will be ready tomorrow." Elaine said to him as she joined her mother.

"Thank you, Sir Alex." Lilith said again, stepping out of the office.

"You said that already. Just get back to your work and keep things going smoothly." He grumbled. "Oh, and Lilith?"

"Yes?"

"Dress the child in blue, not that scullery looking cloth. Fiona's childhood clothing ought to fit her well enough and should not be wasted in closets. You can have those for her. I will not be seen walking in my own garden with a rag-a-muffin."

That had been years ago, before Sir Alex got sick. Now Lilith had to keep reminding her daughter that the man who had been her friend could not walk with her anymore and never would again. She had to explain that he would never be able to be who he was before, and she was trying to find a way to explain the impending death to a child who had no concept of loss. Thanks to the knight there had never ben anything important that Elaine had known the lack of.

What would happen to them now?

If Lionel married Moira or any of the other local girls where would she and Elaine be able to go? They would not want a woman in their household that their husband had once been so close with. Especially if the wedding was forced upon the young knight against his own desire. They would never trust her, and Lilith would hate for their insecurities to ruin Lionel's chance for a good marriage even if it were not going to be a love match.

None of the men who had been suggested as a husband for Fiona were willing to take an unwed mother into their households, they were too deeply entrenched in the teachings and beliefs of the new church to allow such a person to be attached to their name, even as a servant. This meant that, once again, Lilith was out of options and that the happiness she had worked so hard to create for her daughter was in jeopardy. There was no one to swoop in and save her, save them, this time.

"Do not give up just yet, Lilith." The cook said as she loaded the trays with the different breakfast plates. "There are a pair of very handsome knights up there that young Lionel brought with him. You never know if one of them might have need of a wife down south. I heard that Redbourne is a nice place to be. Sir Liam, that man is quite the dish. I cannot say that I would mind being in his kitchen on a daily basis."

"You met The Silver Knight? I heard so many stories about him and Lancelot and the King and the quests they used to go on. There were adventures and battles, foreign courts, and fights. He even saved Lancelot in at least two of the tales." Lilith said with a smile. "Somehow I managed to forget that Lionel serves with the same man that is the legendary warrior."

"He was here, once, with Sir Kay on a mission to the far North. That was when Sir Lionel was quite young, Miss Fiona was still in the nurse's care. It was an incredible few days and the knights were as incredible twenty-years ago as they are now." The cook said with a dreamy look in her eyes. "I must say that it is a wonderful thrill to have a few of them here under this roof again. You should bat your eyes at them a little, flirt. Let those men know that you are available. It cannot hurt to try a little, can it?"

"No, it cannot hurt. In fact, it might spark a touch of jealousy in Lionel. It might be amusing if nothing else. To see how he reacts if someone else, one of his friends, were to flirt with a childhood friend he once shared affection with. It would be useful in helping to convince him to let me leave this place with him and Fiona. To help me with a new beginning."

Lilith picked up the breakfast trays for Lionel and the knights, Moira would have taken Sir Alex' to him before Lilith got to the kitchen.

"Afterall, it is the least he can do for and old friend. Would you not agree?" She asked with a smile at the cook.

"My dear girl, you are so much more than that. Make him see it."

Chapter 10

Lionel had not been home a full day and he already wanted to leave. After the morning meal he had gone to speak more with his father. Intending to find out more about the estate and how it had been running the last few years since he had gotten sick, it had turned into a lecture on how he should stay and look after the estate himself. His father did not understand, or simply refused to consider, that his son did not want the quiet life of a lord in a castle. He was a knight, young and full of adventurous spirit. He still wanted to make his mark on the world and was not ready to settle into the stagnant life of running an entire estate.

It was bad enough to be managing the accounts at Redbourne so that he could, one day, do the same at home. He had no desire to set aside the sword and hide in the North and he had tried to tell his father that.

"There is no joy for me here father. I am not saying that I will never come back to lead the people and accept the mantle of Lord of Scotsbane, but not yet. I am not ready. I have so much more to accomplish before I do that."

"Life is not about joy. Do you not understand, boy, that this is your task. It falls to you, or your sister's husband and I do not want to die knowing that my lands will be run by a stranger that does not understand the people and how things are done here." His father barked, slapping his hand down on the table.

Even old, feeble, and dying his father was a terrifying. It took everything Lionel had to not turn and walk away. The child in him wanted to run but the knight was going to stand firm. He was going to stand up to the old man at last.

"That does not mean that I have to get married father. I can have someone run the estate and take care of the daily management." Lionel said. "I do not have to do this, and I do not want to."

"If you refuse to marry then the estate passes to Fiona at my death and she will then marry Baxter." His father said with a shrug that gave his sister's life away to a man only three years younger than her father. "He is familiar with the way things need to be done here and is eager to make your sister his wife."

"Does that fact not concern you, father?" Lionel bellowed. "That your friend wants to wed and bed your daughter? Your child? Think of how long that man has lusted after her? You would give Fiona, the spitting image of my mother, to that disgusting perverted piece of filth? Just to spite me?"

"No. You damned fool. She will marry him to keep all the people that rely on this house for their safety. If you will not look after them then she will make what sacrifices are needed to see them looked after."

"Do you hear yourself father? This is Fiona. My sister, your daughter. How can you give her away like that? For people that will be taken care of by my steward." Lionel was pounding his own fist on the table.

He was trying to get his father to see reason, to see that this was wrong. There was nothing that was going to convince Fiona that she should do this, and Lionel would rather die than be the man who had to drag his sister to the alter in order to marry a man that she did not love. He had seen that sort of thing in Camelot and a few of the surrounding kingdoms. It was deplorable. Liam had put a stop to it on his lands and, now that he was married, his wife Caelia and her handmaid, Lynn, talked to every bride alone before their wedding to make sure that she wanted to go through with it and that no one was forcing her.

It was an amazing and ground-breaking way of doing things. Lionel was proud to be a part of it, even if it was simply recording the woman's wishes on paper for Liam. This treachery of his father's was something that he could never sanction, he would not be party to it.

"I am not getting married and I will not force my baby sister to marry a disgusting old man." He snarled at his father.

"Be careful with your words boy. It looks like that man is about to be your brother-in-law and the lord of your family home unless you come to your senses. You are completely capable of keeping your sister free to wed who she wishes. All you have to do is pick a bride. Moira would be acceptable though Baxter has a daughter that is quite lovely. Ruth is her name I think."

"What? You must be joking. Father, I cannot marry Ruth any more than I can marry Moira. These girls, these women, have been my friends all my life." Lionel shook his head, raking his hand through his hair. The old man had him over a barrel and they both knew it.

"Marrying her would make it impossible for her father to ever marry your sister. That is a plus in your favor." His father said with a catlike grin. "Though Moira is the prettier one and she is more interesting around the dinner table.

Marrying her might hurt the feelings of your sister's whorish little friend though. She seems to think there is more to you than the spineless boy who left here four years ago."

"Lilith? She is no whore and you will not speak of her like that. She is focused on her child's happiness and nothing else, as any decent parent should be." Lionel snapped dismissively. "Her feelings for me have nothing to do with this."

"No. They do not." Alex said with a sudden frown. "That wench…woman has risen as far in life as she ever will. Her own choices have made her unsuitable for anything else but a maid or a whore. You will not even consider her. Moira or Ruth. You will make a choice by Saturday night and the wedding will be Sunday, in the chapel."

"Sunday? That is three days away." Lionel glared at him. "You cannot expect me to make this choice in three days. Even if I were to agree to marry anyone, I cannot make the choice in that time."

"It will either be you at the altar or your sister, Lionel. Make a choice and make it quickly. Now get out and set yourself to the task."

"I hate you for this." Lionel said before storming out of the office and slamming the door behind him, his father's laughter ringing in his ears.

This was such a mistake. To come back before his death was as wrong and dangerous as he thought it might be. The only good that was going to come from this was that he would be able to save Fiona from being forced to marry Baxter. It might mean that he had to walk down the aisle himself, but at least he could save her. It would be easier for him to avoid his wife than it would for her to avoid a man that had been lusting after her for gods knew how long. That brought back the problem of who to choose as his wife.

It did not seem fair to subject Ruth, who had always been a timid, kind girl, to a marriage that was bound to be loveless. He could hardly do the same to Moira either, though at least he knew her. This was going to be hard, hurting one woman so that he could save another from the horror of an arranged marriage. Sometimes it could work. Liam and Caelia were contracted to each other before they had met and, though they still had some problems, the two of them were deeply in love. Perhaps that was because they chose, or at least Liam chose, to enter into it. This would be more like a forced marriage if he went through with it, and he was beginning to see that he had to go through with it.

His father was a monster, to his children, so that he could be a good lord to the people who depended on him beyond these walls.

Lionel wondered if Fiona knew what the old man had planned for her if he failed to live up to their father's demanding expectations again. He had not likely told her, leaving that lovely task for Lionel to do himself.

She would tell him not to throw his life away, of course, but they both knew that he would never let her marry Baxter. She would still be horrified that this was the only solution to the problem of the estate. It their mother was alive this would have been so much easier. She knew how to deal with his father. She was the only person who could convince him to do the right thing and make him think that it was his idea instead of hers.

Lionel needed her here, as he had so many times growing up. She was dead and gone though, which meant he and Fiona would have to find their own way.

"Have you seen my sister?" He asked one of the maids. "The lady Fiona, where does she spend her mornings?"

"I should think she and Lilith would be taking the child for her morning walk in the garden before the day begins, sir." The girl replied with a curtsey. "The three of them do so every morning sir, since Sir Alex became unable to."

"My father used to take Lilith's daughter for walks in the garden? That seems remarkably unlike him." Lionel said, wrinkling his brow in confusion. "Thank you for the information. I will seek her there and find the answers that I am looking for."

The girl blushed when he flashed her a smile and Lionel had to chuckle to himself on the way to the garden. That was not the reaction he used to get from any of the women around Scotsbane. As a child who loved to read and learn he had never been the dashing heroic type that the girls preferred. Liam had taught him swordsmanship and encouraged him to work with the horses at Redbourne to build muscle and stamina, so that he could fight beside them should the king call upon them to do so. The other senior men, Gerard especially, and Hector, before he returned to Camelot with Mark, had spent a lot of time instructing Lionel, Rion, Emrys and Lucas on the rules and manners of court. He could now negotiate and flirt as well as any courtesan and almost as well as he could manipulate the accounting numbers.

Despite still feeling as awkward as he had when he left it was encouraging to know that, whichever woman he married, his wife would not need to be ashamed of him as a knight. He might be an utter failure at his other duties as a husband, the chief being in love with his wife, but he would always be able to put on the show of being the respectable knight.

"Lionel? What brings you out to the gardens so early in the day, dear brother?" Fiona called as he rounded a corner and spotted the trio walking towards him.

Little Elaine had an apple in her hands and seemed quite proud of herself to be carrying it alone. Her mother had a basket full of the fruit so he could only assume that there would be some apple tart for dessert after the evening meal.

"Our father brings me here Fiona. Good morning sister, to you too Lilith." He said, dropping a kiss to his sister's cheek and nodding to Lilith.

"Really? I do not see him with you, Sir Lionel." Lilith retorted with a grin.

"His orders bring me here Lilith." He said, shaking his head to hide the grin brought by her familiar teasing. "Unfortunately, they are not so amusing."

"Good heavens." Fiona giggled. "What on earth could he have commanded so early in the day to make you so serious Lionel?"

"He has commanded me to marry, to choose a bride to take to the alter by Sunday. If I fail to do so, then you will be at that same alter with Lord Baxter exchanging vows that would bind you to that monstrous old man for the rest of his life. Is that serious enough for you Fiona?"

Chapter 11

"What? Lionel that is not funny. Do not joke about that sort of thing. Lord Baxter had been attempting to flirt with me ever since he found out that father is sick." Fiona cried, stopping in the middle of the path.

Lilith took her friend by the hand and frowned at Lionel. Did the man lack all tact and sense of decency? Was that not taught to knights? How could he joke about something so vile as that disgusting man marrying Fiona.

"Lionel, I know that you have been gone a while, but that man is disgusting. He would not be faithful Fiona. He spends as much time as he can flirting and bedding any girl foolish enough to allow him to touch them. If your father is serious about this you cannot let it happen. You must do whatever it takes to stop it." Lilith said, trying to ignore the fact that she was lecturing the soon-to-be lord of house and land she lived on.

"I intend to stop it, Lilith. It will mean giving up my own freedom, but I will not let my little sister be forced to do anything against her will." Lionel said offering his hand to Fiona. "If I can find a man to manage this place for me, for us, will you come to Redbourne with me?"

Lilith's heart stopped in her chest. This could be the chance she needed to get away from everyone who knew about her past. If she and Elaine could leave Scotsbane with Fiona and Lionel then she could tell folks that she was a widow and have a chance to move on in her life instead of being stuck with the monstrous labels that were whispered in her presence.

"Fiona, that is a wonderful opportunity. You can get away from all this. You can have a new beginning, perhaps even in Camelot itself."

Her friend paused, looking skeptical before she turned her eyes to Lionel.

"Is that possible brother? For me to leave here with you and start over? I would like the chance for someone to know me for myself and not as the daughter of the man who controls their rents and their livelihood."

There was so much hope in Fiona's voice that Lilith did not dare ask for the same for herself, not yet. She could trust in her friendship with Fiona, trust that her friend would not forget her and Elaine when the time came to make decisions that would be, somewhat, permanent.

"That has been my goal since I decided to come back." Lionel told his sister with a smile. "I should never have left you behind Fi. I should have fought to bring you with me. You could have served as a lady to the Queen herself if I had. I cannot make that happen now, for reasons that are not mine to explain. I will do the best I can for you though."

Lilith watched the siblings and realized that despite what she had been through in the last few years the two of them, with their position and wealth, had been through things that were so much harder all their lives. When was the last time that they had known love? How much hurt was hidden behind the hope in Fiona's eyes? In Lionel's? What was it like for them to grow up with Alex as their father?

Fiona threw her arms around her brother's shoulder and held on tight. Lilith felt as though she was bearing witness to something much too private even for the eyes of an old friend, but there was nowhere else to go.

"I know you will Lionel. I know that you will never let that man touch me." Fiona said softly, rubbing her hand across her brother's back in an attempt to sooth him. "We will find a wife for you if that is what we must do. I can help. I cannot promise you love, I think that I can suggest a few ladies that would understand that though."

"Father has made his suggestions, which means that he sees it as an order. I can comply with his wishes or defy them, again." Lionel said, looking at Lilith at last. "Any words of wisdom? Or simply horrified at what I must do to protect my sister."

"Lionel, I do not know what I could say that would make this better. It is wrong that he is forcing you to do this, even more so that he would force her." Lilith said, careful to keep her tone respectful instead of letting the passionate horror that she felt flow through her voice. He was going to be the key to her escape, so she needed him to not get angry at her.

"You had to know that the day would come when a marriage would be needed for the sake of Scotsbane. Even if you did not wish for it, there needs to be a marriage in order for there to be a legitimate heir."

He shook his head, released his hold on Fiona and turned to look Lilith in the face.

"Did they not tell you the same when you had Elaine? That you would need a man in order to have any quality of life for the child? Especially a daughter?"

If he had not been correct, or perhaps because of it, her hand itched to slap him, and she could practically feel the words of retort rising from her stomach.

"The last man that I needed was the doctor who delivered Elaine. Any man since has been helpful, appreciated when they did not cause problems for me, but they were wanted, not needed." She picked up Elaine and hugged her close. "The difference between us is that you need a wife to create an heir and I only need a man's last name attached to mine for everyone to think that I am an honorable widow."

"For all your sense of romance I should simply marry you. I know that we would get along, at least when you are not busy running the household with the efficiency of a general." Lionel said with a dry chuckle before he turned to walk Fiona down the path towards the house.

He could not have known that he had just given her a new idea that negated the request she had intended to make. Of course, he did not know that she wanted to make the request or that so much of her future and that of Elaine would depend on his answer. She could never suggest the marriage, even as a joke, but could she refuse it if he brought it up a second time? Could she risk falling in love just to find a husband?

"Mama? Can we go inside now? I want to play." Elaine interrupted her thoughts. "The other knights are going to play with their swords before they go on their horses. I want to watch."

"We can go see them Elaine, of course." She smiled and picked up her daughter.

Walking towards to yard she had to chuckle when the youngster asked innocently.

"Do you think Lionel is going to play too? I think he would play good with a sword. He would not hit fingers."

"He is a knight Elaine, of course he is good with a sword. I do not know if he can best Sir Gerard though. He is a man that has fought in wars, side by side with King Arthur and the rest of the great knights."

"Is he a great knight too Mama?" Elaine asked leaning against the rail to watch the trio of men from Redbourne. "Is Lionel a great knight?"

"I think he will be, someday. Right now, he is still trying to get himself sorted out to be a good man first. There are a lot of things that he has to worry about here at home before he worries about being a great knight." Lilith replied, settling in to watch the match. "Lots of hard things."

"Good morning, Elaine, Lilith." Moira said dropping down in the seat next to Lilith with a catlike grin. "I see you had the same thought as I did, to get in a viewing of their skills before Saffir and Gerard leave for Gore. They will be bringing the royal twins, Prince Banning and Princess Elin, back with them for a visit to Redbourne. I think it would be wonderful to go with them, attend the Princess and making myself available to the Prince too, of course."

"Good morning Moira." Lilith said without taking her eyes of the men warming up for the first match of the morning. "I am sure that the Princess travels with an attendant of her own so I do not know where you get the idea that you would be the one to attend to her needs. As for the Prince I highly doubt that he is looking for a dalliance with a woman who would throw herself at his head like that."

"Who said it would be his head that I throw myself at." Moira said, preening when Saffir smiled towards them. "Besides, there is a good chance that the princes will be officiating my wedding, if he is not the groom."

"What on earth are you talking about Moira?" Lilith asked, a sinking feeling starting to churn in her stomach.

"Nothing. Nothing other than Sir Alex telling me not ten minutes ago that I am his first choice as a wife for his son. Can you imagine that? How utterly fantastic that would be."

"Are you in love with Lionel?" Lilith asked careful to hide the hurt on her voice.

"Love him? Of course not. Such a silly question." Moira laughed, drawing the eyes of all three knights. "I am sure that I will grow fond of him eventually, Lionel is pleasing on the eyes and will make a wealthy husband, but I certainly do not love him. That is just ridiculous."

"Yes, ridiculous. Of course." Lilith said thoughtfully.

Turning her attention back to the men as the trio began a vigorous sparring routine she held Elaine on her lap and wondered what it would be like if she took Lionel up on his jest of a proposal. Would he be a kind man? The father that her daughter had never had? Would Sir Alex hate him for the choice if he made it? Would Lionel hate her eventually?

She could not say for sure that she would be the perfect wife, or even a good one by the standards of the court, but she would be better for him than Moira. After seeing the raw emotion in the eyes of both siblings while they were in the garden Lilith could not let either of them be used for the gain of others again. After the way that their father intended to manipulate them both to get what he wanted for the estate that meant more to him than his children did Lilith could not play a passive part in the scheme.

Moira and perhaps even Sir Alex might say that what Lilith hoped to have happen was a scheme of equal deviousness, but Lilith had no intention of lying or tricking Lionel into any thing. She would tell him, should he ask again, that she did not love him in the sense of the grand romances of legend but that she would do all she could to be a good wife to him if he could find a way to be a good father-figure to Elaine. They might be able to find a way, through their friendship, to make a new type of relationship work. There would be no false expectations or childish daydreams of love. It just might work, at least enough to give Elaine a happy childhood, fool the other knights and those at court when needed.

All she needed now was for Fiona to give her blessing to the idea and for Lionel to bring the matter up one more time. She would not let the chance slip past her again.

Chapter 12

Lionel watched the girls settle down to watch the morning training out of the corner of his eye. He could practically feel Moira undressing him with her eyes. His father must have already told her that he was forcing Lionel to marry and that she was on the list of approved candidates.

The woman would be insufferable now, where she had simply been obnoxiously forward before. If he did not find her naked in his bed tonight it would be a surprise. He had to make a choice as quickly as possible to save his sanity. Ruth was entirely unsuitable, unless she had gotten interesting in the last few years. Fiona had pointed out while they were walking that, while he had been making a joke, Lilith would make a good candidate for him to consider.

She was smart and kind. She knew how to run a household and, when she wanted to, she could display manners as good as any lady of Camelot. Lilith also had Elaine and Lionel was utterly captivated by the child. She was so solemn when he spoke to her, it was like the child was trying to impress him while he was trying to impress her. Lionel wanted to find a way to make the girl smile, perhaps laugh even.

"Lionel, get your head in the match." Ger called, swatting his backside with the flat of his sword. "Is there something on your mind?"

"Or someone?" Saffir teased, winking in the direction of the girls.

"I have to admit that there is a certain little miss upon my mind that I cannot wait to impress." He prepared his blade and assumed an attack stance. "Shall we fight for the favor the golden-haired damsel, gentlemen?"

The other two men grinned and nodded.

"For the lady's honour." Gerard called and began his attack on Lionel just as the little girl and her mother flashed bright and dazzling smiles at the knights.

The steel in their hands sang out in the soft sunshine of the morning and Lionel threw himself into the fight. Blocking, thrusting with a well-placed slash or well-timed parry of the blades of either of his opponents, Lionel was putting his best efforts into the show for little Elaine. The child seemed to be delighted by the efforts as she cheered and clapped from the sidelines. It was, to Lionel, absolutely adorable when she jumped from her mother's lap to cheer as loud as her small lungs could and wave a fistful of ribbons.

Lionel could feel the eyes of all three women on his back. It felt as though there was an archery target hanging from his shoulders. Whether it would be an arrow of cupid or a dart of The Morrigan that would strike he could not tell but strike it would.

"Mind your blade." Saffir cried, pulling Lionel from his thoughts.

He had nearly taken his friend's hand off at the wrist with his distraction.

"Where the devil is your mind, lad?" Ger asked, raising his shield to block a blow. "Your feet may be upon the field, but your thoughts are anywhere but here."

"My apologies. I will speak to the issue when there is more privacy and less of a chance that the others involved will overhear something that will cause feelings to be hurt that I do not intend."

"Others involved? You have been home less than a day and already there are problems with women? You are worse than Rion and Emrys at the Beltane festival. When will you boys learn that chasing skirts is always going to lead to problems?"

"I am not chasing skirts. They are chasing me it would seem." Lionel laughed. "What would a confirmed bachelor like you know of chasing skirts regardless?"

"Enough to teach the pair of you how to do it correctly and avoid the trouble that you seem to have found yourself in once too often."

"I doubt that, I have seen how you talk to women." Saffir said with a laugh as he retook an attack stance. "Some men say it better with a sword. Steel, not flesh."

All three men joined in the laughter and commenced their training with a renewed energy that brought another round of cheers from the youngster and the other women. For more than an hour there was no other sound but that of blade upon blade and the solid thud of steel being blocked by a wooden shield. There was such a comfort and familiarity in both the sound and physicality that Lionel could allow himself to get lost in it, escaping all else around him. It seemed like only moment had passed when Gerard finally called an end to the practice.

"You have our thanks ladies, for being such a wonderful audience." Saffir called across the yard with a bow as Ger and Lionel gathered the spare weapons.

"Now we ask that you excuse us for now. We must tend to our weapons and wounded pride."

Once they were within the barn, and far from the eyes and ears of the women, Gerard turned to Lionel.

"You have had plenty of time to ponder whatever it was that had you acting like your head was up your ass. Spill it. What is wrong with you?"

"I have to get married." Lionel said with an air of defeat that he could not hide from his friends. "I have to get married in three days or my father is going to force Fiona to marry his best friend, who is at least the same age as he is, if not older."

"What? You cannot be serious? She's a child. Even I did not flirt with her, much." Saffir said before scooping water over his head.

"He is serious and so I must be as well. His suggestions, which are more like orders, are Ruth, the daughter of the man he intends to sell my sister's virtue to, or Moira. I have no idea why her other than that he likes her more than he likes Lilith."

"What is his issue with Lilith? The widow is at least interesting." Ger said.

Lionel knew that he could not be the one to tell Lilith' secret, even to his friends. Her social dishonor was not his story to tell.

"I could not tell you. Perhaps it is because he thinks she can only birth girls and he wants to ensure that the bloodline is carried on through a male heir." Lionel shrugged.

"It has been the path of the female bloodline for centuries and now that he is invested in the teaching of the new church he is pretending that everything else does not exist."

"Or is backwards and barbaric?" Ger added. "Banning, Prince Banning, said something similar in the last letter I had from him."

"It seems as though the older generation is turning away while we hold fast." Lionel said, looking out the back of the barn and across the land. "We have to, or no one will remember."

"Maybe your father simply wants you to marry a pretty, though simple, woman so that your life is a little less complicated. It might mean that it is a boring life, at least outside the bedroom. Simple girls tend to be more compliant between the sheets." Saffir said with a grin.

"Oh, for god's sake, still your tongue Saffir. Lionel, if you must wed for the sake of your father or the safety of your sister then marry someone you can have a conversation with.." Ger grumbled as he oiled the blade of his sword. "I know that you young lads think that beauty, passion, and all the trappings of romance are the most important things in this sort of thing. Trust me, there are things that are much more important."

He sat down and made sure that both of the younger knights were paying attention to him.

"Marry your best friend. You will find that they are the most beautiful creature you have ever seen and that will unleash a passion unlike anything you could experience with someone else."

"I never supposed that you knew or cared much for love." Saffir said, drying his dark curly hair with a towel.

"More than you." Gerard laughed. "I may not leave a string of broken hearts and angry fathers behind me everywhere I go, but that does not mean I have not known love greater than anything you two have yet experienced."

Lionel simply nodded his agreement and wondered if the love that Gerard was waxing poetically about was shared with Liam. The two men had served together for over a decade and Caelia had confided to Lionel the morning after she married Liam that she suspected that her new husband and the blacksmith were secretly lovers. It was also possible that Ger was referring to the Prince of Gore, one of the royal twins he and Saffir were going to bring to Redbourne. The night of the wedding Lionel had been escorting the new lady of Redbourne when they had stumbled upon the knight and the prince in a passionate embrace.

"Love is all well and good, Ger. I do not think that Lionel is going to find that in three days time so that he can marry for love, save his sister and appease his father all in one act." Saffir said, reaching for his shirt which let Lionel and Gerard see his scar covered back.

"The least important of those is pleasing your father though, am I right?" Ger asked.

"Yes. I do not care about how he feels. I would like the woman I marry to understand, to accept, that this is a marriage of necessity and not love. If the feeling grows eventually that is fine but I do not want to lie to her, whoever she is, about my feelings."

"You mean lack of feelings." Saffir said, pulling on his shirt and turning towards the door. "My vote is that you marry Lilith, or at least ask her first. She can cook, hold a conversation and that little girl is something special. Even Ger likes Elaine and I have never seen him like a child before."

"I like children plenty." Ger said, sliding his sword into its sheath at his side. "I work with them every day."

"Very funny. We should get on with the day. When do you two leave for Gore?" Lionel asked as they walked towards the house.

He wanted to ask them to stay, to help him make a choice. They would all have to live with whatever choice he made, and he wanted it to be the right one. It might be a part of his childhood conditioning coming back to haunt him, but he did not trust himself to make the right choice without the opinion of the others. It was not a decision that he could undo either. This was going to be something he had to commit to for the rest of his life so she had to be someone that he could live with too.

"Who do you think I should ask, Ger?" Lionel asked as he got in step with the senior knight. Despite his uncertainty about some of the blacksmith's choices he still held the man in high regard and respected his opinion.

"I cannot tell you that Lionel. If I do and I am wrong then it is my fault. I have no desire to be the reason that you are miserable with the wrong wife. I saw that with Liam the first time, though she did not live long enough for him to see it too." Ger said, shaking his head.

"What if you are right though? What if your suggestion leads me to the woman who can be the wife I need, maybe even make one or both of us happy?" Lionel replied, hoping that he would not have to beg for an answer.

"That could be even worse." He said, stopping outside the main doors. "If that were the case then you would wonder if you would have picked her without my suggestion. That kind of question in the back of your mind would not be good for your happiness either."

"So, you are telling me...what?" Lionel said with a sigh. He was fairly certain that he already knew the answer.

"I am telling you that you have to talk to them, all three of them, and make a choice. Remember what I said in the barn though, marry the one you think you can be friends with when the romance and the passion fade. Marry your friend." Ger said then turned and walked into the house, leaving Lionel in the yard with his thoughts.

Chapter 13

Marry his friend.

If only it was that easy to do. Moira had been his friend for years, but the idea of being married to her just did not sit right. Part of him felt as though he would always have to wonder who the father of their children was if he married her. She was a woman of passion, with needs and if he went to war with the king or on a quest with the knights he could not swear that she would not fill her desires elsewhere. As beautiful as she was, and despite being a friend of his younger days, he could not see himself being a happily married man with a woman whose fidelity was questionable.

Ruth, the other option approved by his father, barely more that a stranger to him. She was a few years younger than Fiona and he remembered attending a ball, shortly before he left, that announced her entrance to society. He may have danced with her, but Lionel could not remember a single word that she had said. How could he marry her, or even ask to marry her, if he barely remembered her?

The options presented by his father were less and less appealing the longer he considered them and Lilith, with her sarcasm, honesty, and unique situation, was becoming more and more appealing. His father would hate the idea, thus giving it a greater appeal, but how was he going to convince her to accept him? She was proud and independent, fully capable of doing anything she needed without the help of a man. That was as appealing as it was difficult to work around.

How did he convince a woman who did not need a man to marry him?

"Sir Lionel?" One of the servants called from the door. "Your father has guests waiting for you, Sir Baxter and his daughter Ruth."

"He could not let me do this my way. Even when I talk to these women is not allowed to be my choice." He muttered to the sky.

A few minutes later Lionel walked into the hall where his father was sitting, propped up with pillows, on his great chair where he would deal out judgements and address complaints from the tenants in years gone by. Standing near it was a towering brute of a man that Lionel recognized immediately as Sir Baxter, which made the petite girl beside him Ruth.

She was as dainty looking as he remembered. Her hair the same rich gold as daffodils and when she lifted her chin her eyes were a bright blue, sad and defeated as well. It hurt his heart to stare into them and know that he would not be the hero to save her from the life she was trapped in. As she watched him approach with hope growing in her expression Lionel wished that he could be what she needed, but he needed a practical woman and not a damsel in distress that would fall in love with him.

"Lionel, Sir Baxter and his lovely daughter Ruth heard this morning that you have come home. They have come to welcome you home and see that you are properly introduced to Ruth. She is of an age to marry you know, son."

"Yes father, so you informed me of not more than a few hours ago, as soon as I woke." Lionel said, trying to hide the annoyance in his voice. "Hello again, Sir Baxter. Ruth, the last time I saw you I believe it was at a dance in your honor. My apologies if you had to suffer through any of my clumsy footwork. I had not yet learned to dance properly."

Baxter nodded to him "You have been away too long, young man. There are things here that have needed your attention. It is high time you made things right and accepted your responsibilities."

"I accepted them long ago. There were simply things that needed my attention more than an estate with more than one capable and competent man." Lionel shook his head then turned to smile at Ruth who beamed up at him. This was already trouble.

"I am sure that you were more than capable as dancer, Sir Lionel." She said with a pretty blush rising on her cheeks.

Dear god, what had they told her about him already that he was going to have to disillusion her about.

"That is kind of you, but I promise that I was likely horrible since I still am."

"Why not take the young lady for a stroll in the garden Lionel? Get to now each other again?" Sir Alex said with a preening smile. "I am sure that she would love to see them."

"Just as much as I am sure that you have exaggerated their attributes to a level of unrealistic expectation." Lionel said with a glare before offering his arm to the young woman. "I would, of course, be honored to escort you. If you are actually interested in the flowers, that is."

"I would greatly enjoy that, thank you."

He groaned inwardly when she blushed again and took his arm. This was going to be worst than kicking a puppy. This girl was one of the those that read poetry and romance to keep herself occupied. She likely expected flowers and equally descriptive words of devotion that he would not be capable of even if he did have feelings for her. If this were her first foray into the reality of love then it was going to be rougher than it should be, but he would not lie to her and he would not give her false hope where there was none.

"What kind of flowers do you favor Ruth? Perhaps my sister has some planted." Lionel asked as they slowly strolled the path.

"I would have to say roses, they look the loveliest in a bridal bouquet I think. Would you agree?" She asked, stopping to inspect one of the bushes closer.

"I would have to leave that to you ladies to decide such thing. I have not given much thought to marriage. It is not something I had considered for myself until my father reminded me that it was necessary to maintain a firm hold on the estate for the family. Either my sister or I must provide an heir. He has decided that it will be me, at least who marries first." Lionel shrugged and ran his eyes over the carefully groomed garden. "It was not my idea or my choice."

He turned to look at Ruth and watched her understanding of what he had said wash over her face. She grew serious for a brief moment, the bright smile fading from her lips. Before he could say anything else she simply tilted her head and held out a hand to him.

"There are times when it is best to follow tradition and make the best of it afterwards. Many things can be improved or mended after the fact."

"As true as that may be, Ruth, there are many other things that cannot be forced or faked. Those are the things that a marriage can be built on. Without them we would simply be kidding ourselves and could never be happy." Lionel said with a deep sigh.

"Never Lionel?" She asked, her eyes wide and saddened.

"Never Ruth. It would not be possible."

He took her hand, tucked it into his arm and continued the walk. They talked about the garden and a few stories from Camelot.

"It all sounds so wonderous and adventurous. I wish that I could see it, be a part of it." Ruth said wistfully. "It would be amazing to see Camelot in all it's glory. The king and queen, all the knights and ladies in their court attire."

"Then why not go and see it? I would think that if you wrote to the Queen and told her of your desire to see the capital she would respond with an invitation. She is fond of her ladies and enjoys hearing stories of the different parts of the land." Lionel suggested, hoping that perhaps it would be a decent consolation after the marriage rejection.

"Do you think she would? My father could hardly refuse an invitation from the Queen herself. I have never been south of Scotsbane before."

"I am not surprised. The men of our father's generation are not known for their open minds or love of travel. I am fairly certain that the invitation would come. Arthur might even summon your father to court as well."

As he expected, the expression on Ruth's face sank to a cautious reservation. He suspected that the young girl was anxious to have an adventure without the formidable countenance of her father hanging over her shoulder.

"I am not sure that he would want to leave his estate in the care of a steward simply to indulge in a social visit, even one of such significance."

Lionel chuckled at her naivety. There was not a lord or knight of the realm that would refuse the direct invitation of the High King of England.

"I think you will find that he would be as eager to attend the city as you are Ruth. He would need to be there to give his consent to any proposals or engagements, of which I am certain you would have many."

The return of her smile and the blush on her cheek told Lionel that this was just what she needed. The dream of a palace romance, sneaking under the eye of her father until some brave and smitten man was bold enough to make a proposal. Such things were the daydream of every country maiden, whether her father was a lord, knight, or peasant farmer. They all wanted the same thing: romance.

Romance that led to weddings and babies and eternal bliss. That is what women wanted, what their mothers and nursemaids taught them to want and what their fathers expected young men to provide even though they did not do the same when it was themselves at the alter. Lionel had to find a woman who had no such wish or expectation. That was the only way that this was going to work without breaking several hearts and earning him the hatred of a father-in-law and, quite probably, his own wife.

Escorting Ruth back to the hall where their fathers were waiting, Lionel could not help a small amount of smugness when he bowed in farewell.

"Thank you for a lovely conversation. I do hope that the invitation you hope for comes soon and yields the results you desire." He gave a chaste kiss to the back of her hand and straightened. "Perhaps by then my wife and I will be able to extend you an invitation to visit us at Redbourne."

He was not sure which was more amusing, the look on Baxter's face when he realized that Lionel was going to marry someone else or his father's when he heard that his son was not going to stay at Scotsbane.

"If you will all excuse me my friends are getting ready to leave. They are heading north, to Gore. The royal twins have accepted an invitation for Prince Banning to come and train with Liam and the rest of the knights at Redbourne."

Ruth smiled at him and took her place beside her father.

"I think it would be lovely to come and see you there. When you make that choice, I am sure that she will be a lucky woman. I hope that you find the happiness you want along with all those things that you said you cannot marry without. Best of luck to you, Sir Lionel."

He gave the trio a nod, took his leave of them and the hall. He had to see them off and remind them to hurry their return. His father would not last much longer and, if there was to be a wedding on Sunday, Lionel wanted to take his bride as far away from this place as soon as he could. There was no more joy to be found at Scotsbane for him and he was tired of trying to pretend that there was.

Chapter 14

"I do not know why you are concerning yourself with this Lilith. Lionel is going to choose me, and we will be married on Sunday." Moira said, fluffing her hair.

Lilith had made the mistake of telling Moira what Lionel had said to her and to Fiona in the garden. The other woman had laughed viciously at the idea that the heir to the estate would marry the single mother, despite his own words on the subject.

"You do not know that. He could choose Ruth. Lord knows that girl is a perfectly chaste bride and obviously has Sir Alex's approval." Lilith countered, as angry at Moira as she was at herself for trusting her with the confidence of the conversation.

"As do I, he did tell me that himself." Moira countered. "Which is more than you can say. I would dare to suspect that you are not on the approved list at all, let alone near the top. Despite what Lionel says, he will need his father's approval for his wife."

"His own choice will override his father. If you knew him as well as you think you do, then you would know that."

"Well, then I will simply have to settle for knowing him biblically then, will I not? Besides if he does not ask me then I can simply tell his father about our tryst and there will be no other choice. By the law of the church he will have to marry me." Moira said with a catlike smile. She quickly adjusted her bosoms to sit as high in her gown as possible without showing the edge of her nipples.

"I suppose that it is lucky, for Lionel, that he and the king both still follow the old religion which frees him from that responsibility." Lilith said before she left Moira alone with the realization that her trap would not work unless Lionel wanted it to work.

"Please let him be smart enough to not choose that disaster waiting to happen as a bride. She thinks too much like his father." Lilith whispered to the sky.

"Who is too much like my father?" Lionel said with a smile that looked forced.

He surprised her by rounding a corner and stepping into the hallway beside her.

"Moira." Lilith answered, stealing a quick look over her shoulder to make sure that the other woman had not come out of the room yet. "She follows the new religion, at least in word. There are some aspects of it's laws that she finds appealing and useful in her search for a husband."

"Ah, I see." Lionel replied, offering her his arm. "Will you let me walk you to wherever it is that you need to go?"

"Oh. Thank you. I was just going to check on Elaine. She is usually quite good at occupying herself and staying out of trouble, but with the other knights causing such a buzz amongst the staff she is determined to see as much of them as possible." She did not know what it was about Lionel that made her so comfortable talking about Elaine. She rarely mentioned her daughter to men, and even rarer was a man that was interested in the doings of a child, whether it was his own or not.

"Well then perhaps after they leave I can help to stave off her disappointment by spending some time with her? Horse riding? Perhaps let her try on some armor?" He flashed her a grin. "Would you object to sword training? With a stick of course."

She wanted to laugh at his eagerness. For a man who had Sir Alex as a paternal influence Lionel had the potential to be an incredible father. She wondered what it would be like to raise a child with someone who wanted to be a family. With someone who would stay.

"I would warn you to watch your fingers but that would be my only caution for that plan." Lilith said with a small laugh. "She is definitely her mother's daughter and has a bit of a wild side already."

"There is nothing wrong with that." Lionel replied. "Perhaps the steadying influence of a father figure would be good for her. Have you ever considered a marriage? I know you are independent, but it might make a few things easier for you."

"That is the second time today you have mentioned marriage to me Lionel. You had best be careful or I might start to think you are serious about this." She said with a smile.

Opening the door to the room she was allowed to use as a nursery for Elaine, Lilith could not help but laugh to see her daughter using a stick to attack the chairs that went around the table. She was swinging hard and fast at the wooden villain, all in defence of the pillow wearing one of Lilith's sashes as a dress.

"I am not sure if a father would steady her or add to her wildness. To answer your question though, no. I do not think I have considered marriage. Honestly, I have doubted that another man would want to take on both of us, at least any of the men around here."

"Have you considered relocating if no one here is willing to see how wonderful Elaine is? How wonderful you both are?" Lionel asked seriously when they had closed the door and continued down the hallway. "Camelot has many widows with children, and they do not seem to have much issue finding company or husbands if they choose it. Even around Redbourne there are men with more open minds and hearts."

"Are you one of those men Lionel? Or are you simply trying to convince me to come with your sister when you take her away from here?" Lilith asked.

She was skeptical of something that sounded so good, too good. Nothing in life came easily and the idea that the knighted son of a lord would be interested in her or that the men who kept company with one of the greatest knights of the realm would want to marry a single mother, widowed or not, seemed to be better than anything she had ever seen or heard of outside the pages of romantic tales.

"I am most definitely one of those men, Lilith. Was that not clear this morning when I spoke of marriage to you." Lionel said, stopping her next to the stained-glass window that was sending beams of red and gold to the wall behind them.

This could not be happening, not like this. It was ridiculously romantic and there were too many things that needed to be talked about before such a commitment could be made.

"I thought you were simply speaking to a friend. I did not think that you were serious." She said stepping back out of the light. "A proposal without a discussion about our expectations of each other would be foolish. We have not had any such discussion so I would not think that you would be serious about a proposal until that had occurred."

Lilith almost laughed at the shock on Lionel's face. He had actually thought that she would simply fall at his feet and let him break traditions as well as tie herself to a man before she had made sure that her daughter would be well cared for. He was a fool if he thought that she was desperate and even more so if he thought she was not just as smart as he was.

"My parents loved each other very much and their marriage was a wonderful example of the work such a relationship takes to make it a success. I intend to have something as close to what they had as possible." Lilith said, trying to keep her voice calm as she locked eyes with Lionel.

It was hard not to get lost in the bright blue gaze now that she knew Lionel was watching her, focussing on her alone. This must be how so many women lost their minds, hearts, and honor. It would be so easy to succumb to him if he were bent on a seduction. She already found herself wondering what it would be like to kiss him, to be held in those strong arms that swung a sword with as much ease as her daughter swung a birch switch. What kind of lover had studious young Lionel grown up to be? If he were serious about his intentions then she would find out in just three days time. Staring back at him it was hard not to lose her concentration and her train of thought was definitely slipping.

"I want that kind of marriage too Lilith. If I have to marry then I want it to be with a partner, not someone who is looking for a life of luxury. I want to work towards something, build something. I need someone who has the strength and determination to match mine. I think you are the only woman I know who has that capability."

"Yet a marriage is still something that you must be forced to do. What romance is there in that for a woman? What hope for happiness?" Lilith said with a sudden frown. "Excuse me Lionel I have things to see to. If you are getting married in three days, we servants have our work cut out for us getting things ready."

She turned to walk away, confident that her words would remind him of the difference between them. He could marry, put some effort into it and if it did not work out how he liked he could put his wife aside and try again or he could take a mistress. Someone in the position that Lilith lived every day could not afford to take the risk of a man who was looking for a bride, not a wife, but a bride simply to appease the demands of his father. She had to make a better choice, a solid choice with some kind of guarantee that would at least protect Elaine even if it did not protect her or her heart.

She thought that she had left him behind on the landing but as she rounded the corner of the staircase a firm hand grabbed hold of her arm above the elbow and spun her back around. Before she could say a word Lionel's hand was cupping her cheek and his lips crashed down over hers.

His kiss was firm, as possessive as it was passionate. His fingers threaded into her hair, loosening it from the ribbons that kept it from falling over her face. It had been so long since a man had kissed her that Lilith was taken aback in surprise and when the tip of his tongue slid along the crease of her lips she resisted the urge to open them just long enough to make him press harder. The moan that slipped from her throat was one of such hunger that she felt the heat of a blush rise on her cheeks and Lionel smiled against her lips.

"My apologies. I could not bear the thought of you living a life without romance and that was the most romantic thing that I could think of." Lionel said with a grin as he held out the ribbon from her hair that had caught in his fingers. "I do not want you think that I am offering you a life without romance or the hope for love, Lilith. That is not my intent."

"Then what is your intent Lionel? To have a little fun? Inspire my dreams only to send them crashing to the ground when you marry Moira because your father approves?" Lilith asked, staring up at him while she quickly tied her hair back in an attempt to hide what had just happened. "What do you want from me?"

"I will say it again, then later we will talk and discuss the details since you do not have a father living that I can ask. Lilith, I want you to marry me and I want for you and Elaine to come back to Redbourne with me and Fiona. I want to start a new life with you, satisfy my father's dying command and, most of all, I want you to fall in love with me."

Chapter 15

Lionel did not know what had come over him. Watching Lilith walk away, her words putting a wall between them that he did not know how to break through, he had to stop her. He could not explain why it meant so much to him that she saw herself as living in such a different world than he did, that he was not capable of romance and that a marriage to him would be one without hope for love.

That was not what he wanted. He wanted her to be excited about his proposal, about a life together. He wanted her to want to fall in love with him, to let him be a part of a family with her and Elaine, maybe more children of their own too. Lionel had thought that the way to get to her, to get her to agree, would have been to be blunt and honest. She did not strike him as someone who craved romance and yet she walked away when she thought that there was none to be found with him.

That was when he rushed down the steps to kiss her as he had never kissed a woman in his life. There was no intention of game playing or subtle flirtation in that that kiss. It was a kiss of pure possession. The kind that a man gave only to the woman he wanted above all others.

Damn it all, he was going to find a way to make her want him, to get her to agree. No one else was going to be the right match for him, certainly not Moira or Ruth. He had barely more than two days to convince her to marry him, tell his father, which would mean dealing with his anger, and then getting the ceremony together in a way that was acceptable to everyone involved. With Ger and Saffir leaving this meant that he had no ally in his seduction and no co-conspirator to help him win the interest, if not the heart, of his bride to be.

He could not do this on his own.

Fiona.

His sister might be able to help, at least with calming their father. First he would need to let her in on his intention, then beg for her help or her advice. It benefitted her too so he was fairly certain that she would be more than willing to help him. Confident in his success Lionel made his way to Fiona's room where his sister was reading a letter on the window seat.

"You look even deeper in thought than I am sister. Something troubling you?" Lionel asked with a concerned smile. "May I see the letter? Who sent it?"

"Lionel, this was left by Sir Baxter. He is telling me of his plans for our life together if you do not find a bride for Sunday." His sister said forlornly. "He is disgusting in his descriptions. I cannot go there. I cannot live that life. Please, big brother, save me. Take me with you when you leave this place."

"I intend to do a little bit better than that, little sister." Lionel said, holding out his hand for the letter.

If Baxter were being crude and cruel to his sister that would be one more thing that he needed to deal with before leaving Scotsbane after his father died. It took reading only a few lines before Lionel was enraged and disgusted with the flowery script that was designed to hide the atrocities that were the contained on the pages. He wanted to burn it, destroy all evidence and consequence of the words. This was the kind of letter that scarred a soul and the soul that it was trying to ruin was the one that belonged to his sister.

"Forget about this letter. I am going to deal with Baxter tomorrow when I go to tell him that I will not be marrying his daughter and he will never, ever, get to talk to you again." Lionel said firmly as he wrapped his arms around Fiona. "I am going to beat them at their own game, little sister. I just need your help to convince Lilith to marry me."

"Absolutely not Lionel. You cannot marry her. I should say you will never be able to convince her to marry you, not when she knows that you do not want to marry anyone."

"Why not?" Lionel protested. "I am decent looking, more than well off, financially, and I will take care of her and Elaine. I doubt that a matchmake in the court could make a better argument for it."

"She is not going to settle for someone who does not love her. Really love her." Fiona said. "Lilith did that once and that is how she got Elaine. Do you really think a woman who looks like her has not been proposed to before? She is beautiful, funny, and smart. Any and every single man in the area has tried to convince her to settle down with them. They offer her such practical things as security and accepting Elaine, so she knows that she can get those things regardless of who she might choose. She wants love Lionel. To be wooed and adored. To feel as though she is the only woman you can imagine yourself with for the rest of your life."

"So, she wants romance? I can give her romance." Lionel said smugly. This would be easy enough now that he knew what she wanted from him.

"Lionel? Can you give her romance and mean it? Or at least intend to mean it?" Fiona said, crossing her arms and looking him in the eye. "If you cannot, or will not try, then do not try to make her believe that you will because all you will do is break her heart and yours. That is not fair to either of you."

"I cannot promise anything Fiona, except that I will do whatever I can to save you from the results of my failure." Lionel said, frustrated that not even his sister believed that he was capable of loving someone as special as Lilith. Had he been so cold when he was younger that it seemed impossible for him to love? "I want to find love Fi, I do. There has just never been anyone who has inspired me to fall. What is wrong with me?"

"Oh brother." Fiona crossed the room to wrap her arms around his ribs. "There is nothing wrong with you except that you have not met the right person at the right time. You are a good man. You just need to open up and take a risk with your heart."

"The time for risks is over and I am out of time to weigh the options. It is either Lilith or Moira. Father's bargain with Baxter has seen to the end of my choices. I cannot and will not marry Ruth." Lionel sat on the edge of Fiona's bed, just like when they were young and trying to come up with a plan that would keep one or both of them out of trouble.

"If you truly must choose now, with no other option waiting for you at Redbourne, then Lilith is the better woman and would make a good wife and mother. If you can win her heart that is." Fiona said sitting next to him. "Oh, I have an idea. If you want to win Lilith's heart and show her that you are serious then you need to win over Elaine first."

"Elaine? Why?" Lionel could not understand what the interest of a child was going to do to influence this situation.

"Lionel, do you not remember what mother used to say about us? What she used to call us?"

"You mean, other than trouble and mischief?" He grinned. "She used to say that we were her heart walking around before her eyes. Her heart. Of course."

There was no way that Lilith would marry a man that did not have the approval and affection of her child. That was how he could show her that he was serious about his proposal and their future.

"It may not be the answer, but it is the start that I needed. Thank you Fiona." He stood and went to the window so that he could see the garden below. "I will go and find the little one and see if I can get on her good side. It cannot hurt to try, can it?"

"I think that it is the gateway to what you want. If Elaine does not like you then you may have to reconsider Ruth as an option if Moira really is unacceptable." Fiona laughed. "Why is that, by the way, that you do not want to choose her? You have already known her intimately. If father knew that he would force you to marry her, you know that."

"I do not follow this new religion of rules and control so he can say whatever he wants. I am not going to marry her because, though there is the lingering affection of childhood friendship I do not like her especially. I was not the first man that shared her bed and though that does not bother me, a woman can do as she likes in that regard, I did not like that she reminded me of the same thing that you did. That she could have me forced to marry if she wanted to. She uses her body to try and trap men. I do not want to feel trapped in my marriage any more than is already happening."

Fiona stared at him. "My gods. No wonder you are so opposed to her and to marriage in general. From the very first-time women have been trying to trap you and now, ironically, you are trying to trap Lilith."

"I am not trying to trap her. I am trying to give her a good life, an even better life for her daughter and the hope for love as we grow together. Is that not enough? Is that not more than most of us can hope for in this kind of situation?" Lionel said.

"There is nothing wrong with that, brother, but she is going to want love and I doubt that she will settle for less than her heart's desire. I think you will find that there is more feeling in her heart and your own if you stop worrying about father or his declaration and think about Lilith. How do you feel when you think of her?"

He paused and considered the question. Lilith was physically beautiful, that was without a doubt. She had big eyes the colour of dark amber with thick black lashes framing them above her freckled little snub nose. Her hair was long, to her waist at least, shiny, thick and the color of buckwheat honey. When he had tugged if free of the ribbons that tied it back Lionel had been delighted with how soft it was. Her body was a paradise of curves that called out to have his hands caress them, kiss them, and commit them to memory, but that was not what had made him want to marry her.

"Lionel?" Fiona called him back to the moment. "How do you feel about Lilith?"

"I think that she is the most courageous woman I know. Intelligent, beautiful, hard-working, and so strong. I would be the luckiest man in Briton if she agreed to be my wife." He said with a grin that came so suddenly his face hurt.

"Then remember that when you see her next, when you talk to Elaine, which you should do soon and within sight but not earshot of her mother or one of the other ladies. That part is important, trust me." Fiona said with a serious expression.

"Little sister, I will be the picture of decorum. I promise." He said, placing a kiss on her forehead. "We will have a new life soon, all of us. You can marry whoever you choose, and we will be happy far, far from here."

"Nothing would make me happier, big brother." She beamed up at him, making him feel like a hero. "Now, go and do this right so that I can have a sister in a few days."

Chapter 16

Lionel was rushing through the halls, trying to get to the garden where Elaine was playing before she was taken inside, or her mother arrived. It was important, now that he had a goal in mind, that he acted quickly to secure it successfully. After all, a woman could not be that different than the sums he calculated to manage the estate at Redbourne or more resistant to success than a strategy for battle. He could definitely win her over now that he had a plan.

Once he reached the garden Lionel slowed down, doing his best to make his pace calm and casual. There was no need for Elaine to know that he had come looking for her, that would ruin any chance for an authentic interaction.

Once he found the girl, playing in the bushes with one of the maids from the kitchen nearby watching, he did his best to try and remember what it was like to be a child, innocent and carefree. He had no clear memories of such a time for himself, but he could remember Fiona at this age.

"Good afternoon, Lady Elaine. Are you hunting for the fairy folk in the bushes? My sister Fiona used to the very same thing when she was your age." He said to her, lifting up a branch to see her face.

"Did she ever catch one?" Elaine asked, crawling out from beneath the bush and standing up straight to look at him.

"I do not know if she ever caught a fairy, but she certainly caught enough spiders and butterflies to drive my father and the house staff out of their minds." He chuckled and snatched a butterfly out of the air by making a loose cage with his fingers. "I always thought it was better to let them go though, to fly in the wild."

Elaine nodded as though he had said something profound that she understood on a level that even he did not.

"Because some things are not meant to be kept locked away?"

"That is certainly a true statement Elaine. There are many wild things that should never be caged in. There are others though that need to be taken care of and the wild is too dangerous for them alone." Lionel said, releasing the butterfly. "The hard part is to know the difference."

"How do you know the difference?" Elaine asked, looking up at him with pure innocent curiosity in her big brown eyes.

Lionel felt a tug on his heart that he had not expected. What was it about this child that brought out his guardian instincts? She was utterly sweet and the way she gazed up at him made him feel like a hero. He felt like he could and would destroy anyone and anything that hurt her or took away even a touch of that innocence. For the first time in his life he understood what it was that made the fathers of daughters so protective.

"Well, I do not always know and sometimes I make mistakes. Trying to protect a wild thing that does not need to be protected, simply admired." He pointed to the butterfly that had stayed close enough to be seen, but not touched. "Sometimes they stay if you are good and kind to them. They stay so that all of their wonderfulness can be enjoyed by those that love them."

"Are you good and kind Lionel? Knights are supposed to be good and kind. That is in the story books." Elaine said, offering him a stick and taking a child's version of an attack stance. "Or a wicked bad knight that is secretly a dragon needing to be slayed?"

"I think slain is the right word, but I definitely am not a dragon. Unless I am cursed by a wicked wizard and need the kiss of a fair maiden to break the curse? Do you know one who could save me?"

The sweet little girl blushed just like her mother, a beautiful pink all the way up to her hair, and she giggled behind her hands while he waited for her to answer him.

"Mama can break the curse. She can do anything."

"You know, Elaine, I think I believe you." Lionel said standing up.

He had that uncomfortable feeling that he was being watched and it did not feel friendly. He scanned the garden in front of him before he turned around and saw a pair of priests walking towards them. The maid from the kitchen was nowhere in sight so it was up to him to deal with them and keep Elaine safe at the same time. There was something about these men with their vows and robes and monasteries that he did not trust, especially around children.

"Lionel. It is good to see you home once again. Here for your father I assume?" One of them said, stepping forward.

Lionel noticed how Elaine quickly hid behind him and immediately felt defensive and protective.

"I do not believe that I know you well enough for such familiar terms or conversation. I am home at the request of my father and will be here for his final days. Then I shall take my family, what remains of it, back to Redbourne with me for a time." He said carefully, keeping one hand behind him, to touch the top of Elaine's head. "Who are you?"

"I am Father Ignatius from the church your father has been attending. Until he became ill of course, that is why I have been visiting him here." The priest said with an annoyingly confident smile on his face. "I have found that this garden is my favorite on the property. So peaceful and well maintained. It would make a wonderful prayer garden for the faithful."

"Then it is a shame that once he is gone you will no longer be visiting it. Perhaps our gardener can help bring your own grounds up to a similar standard."

"You are going to stay and take over for your father then, Lionel? He will be quite pleased. Many of the days that I came here to talk to him it was on his mind, what would happen to the property and the people he has cared for if you chose your life there over your duty." The father said with an audible hint of disappointment in his voice.

There was no doubt in Lionel's mind that the priest and his brothers wanted Scotsbane to add to their own estate. They might claim it to be in the name of their god, but the young knight suspected that there was more greed than grace in their plan.

"I think that there is nothing, other than the funeral for my father, about this estate that needs to concern you ever again." Lionel said, turning slightly when Elain tugged on his sleeve.

He carefully picked up the child and allowed her to wrap her legs and arms around him. He could feel the fear in her grip and wondered what these priests had said or done to make her feel like this.

"All of those that live here, wish to stay here and need to be taken care of will find that their needs are met, and their freedoms are unaltered. Can you offer them the same under your roof?" Lionel asked, wrapping his arms protectively around Lilith's daughter.

"It is the roof of God not of man and he will provide for all their needs. Your bride-to-be believes in what we teach and has already spoken of the great work that we will do together in the years to come."

"My what? Who has told you such a thing?" Lionel snapped, his hand cradling Elaine's head. "I do not and will not follow this new religion. I will find a druid for a true ceremony after the false one for my father's sake."

"The lady Moira has been at the church for the last few weeks planning the ceremony. Was she keeping that a surprise from you? She is a most efficient woman. You are a blessed man to call her your bride." The priest said happily.

"She is not my bride and will not be. I do not care if she is my father's choice I will not marry a woman that wants to dictate every part of my life, especially without my consent." He snarled viciously. "You are not going to add my estate to your church. Not while I am in charge."

The priest stood still, so did his companion, and glared silently at Lionel for a few moments before speaking.

"You should be careful what declarations you make, Sir Lionel. You never know when the laws will change and make what you believe dangerously against the law. The King cannot save you from every mistake you make, and this is one that I will remember."

Lionel gently set Elaine down on the ground and stepped up to the priest. Toe to toe and nose to nose he glared at the man. If he were anyone but a priest there would be no resolution without the violence of a duel, but even a knight in disgrace knew better than to start that fight. It would follow him everywhere he went and those who did not know the darkness that these men were capable of with so much wealth and the secrecy they were afforded behind closed door.

"You can trust that I will remember your words today as well. You had best hope that this is the last time we speak on the subject of my home or my marriage. If it happens again we will have quite the serious problem."

For a brief moment Lionel thought that the priest was going to strike him, which would give him the excuse he needed to put the arrogant piece of clergy in his place and off of his property.

The tension of the moment was broken by the arrival of Lilith.

"Lionel? Have you seen Elaine? The knights are ready to leave and I want to make sure that she has not stowed away somewhere trying to go with them on an adventure."

"She is here with me. We were having a conversation about wild things before we were interrupted." Lionel said, guiding Elaine forward while keeping his eyes on the priests.

"Lilith." Father Ignatius said with the coolness of a snake. "Still living up to your namesake? Or have you decided to join the cloister with your innocent bastard and save both your souls from the damnation of God and the church."

"No deity that loves like you claim that yours does could damn a child born innocent of the actions of it's parents and I do not believe that one anyone, god or man, who truly loves someone would judge and hold their past against them." Lilith hissed angrily, cuddling her daughter protectively and impressing Lionel at the same. "If that is the ultimatum of your god then he is not the right one for the people of Briton and certainly not the one for me."

"Or me." Lionel added, positioning himself. "I refuse to bend to this new religion or acknowledge the power that men claim in the name of their deity."

"You will not speak in vain of the one true God." The priest that accompanied Ignatius said, his face purple with rage.

"And you will not speak in my house, or stand in it, or return to it. Ever." Lionel stepped towards him, rage pulsing through his veins. "If you ever speak to the Lady Lilith, or her daughter, in that way I will see if you enjoy the cross as much as that savior you claim to worship."

"There is no need for threats, Sir Lionel." Ignatius said.

"There is no need for you and yours to insult the woman I intend to marry and the child that will be my daughter. Get out of OUR house, now." Lionel barked, pointing towards the gates. "Out, before I throw you out with my own hands."

He watched them try to walk calmly towards the exit, but it seemed as though they were nearly running. Who could tell beneath those floor length robes.

"I swear, we will never have to deal with them again. My apologies for how they spoke to both of you. I will not tolerate anyone, and I do mean anyone, addressing you like that in the future."

"What are you talking about Lionel? What future is this that you are dreaming up now?" Lilith asked, placing a kiss on Elaine's forehead, and letting her walk ahead on the path a little bit. "I do not know what is going on here."

"What is going on, going badly I might add, is me telling you that I want to marry you. For real, not just a hypothetical or because I have no other option. I think you are the most amazing woman I have ever met. I think your daughter is a gem of innocence. I think that there is no one that I have ever met that who inspires me more than you have since I returned." Lionel said, taking her hands in his and looking down into her eyes. "I know that this is not perfect, perhaps not the kind of romance you want. I promise, if you say yes, I will work on the romance and all the other things you need. I will do as much as I can to be the husband you need, because I think, I know, that you already are the woman I need. Will you marry me the day after tomorrow and spend the rest our lives building something as close to perfection as we can get?"

Chapter 17

Lilith stared at Lionel. It felt as though her world was standing still, frozen, waiting for her to answer the question. She barely understood him at first, but the words slowly became clearer and clearer until she understood the depth of what he was saying, what he was offering her.

She had thought it was sweet that he was spending time with Elaine and was surprised at how aggressively he defended both of them against the priests. Pleasantly surprised. It was the kind of thing that knights did, that heroes did. This knight, this hero, this beautiful man, had stood up for her with no cause or motive and then proposed marriage as though she were the prize and he would be lucky to have her, instead of the reality which was the reverse.

"I..." She looked over his shoulder towards Elaine who was smiling at her happily. "I will. Yes, Lionel, I will marry you."

Lilith expected a nod and, perhaps, a smile to go with the acceptance since they were not in love, but he swept her into his arms and crashed his lips down over hers. It was wildly passionate, even more so than the kiss in the stairwell, the difference was obvious his delight in her response. When she kissed him back Lilith found that she was more excited than she thought she would be. Giving in to the moment she threw her arms around his neck and, for the first time in years, opened herself up to potential passion.

For so long she had been holding back, ignoring that side of herself to avoid further complications. She did not allow men to court her and avoided contact with most of them unless she was involved in a task for Sir Alex. There was just too much trouble when one got involved with a man, her daughter was proof of that. If Lionel stood by even half of what he had just declared then she would have a better life than she could find with anyone here at Scotsbane.

When his hands slid up and down her back, pulling her tight against his chest Lilith was amazed that hands which wielded a heavy sword with such fierce intensity could cradle her so gently. There was so much about Lionel that she did not understand, he was warrior in the presence of the other knights but played with butterflies when he was with Elaine. All his life he had been determined to win the approval of his father, but he had proposed to her with the full knowledge that she was not who the old man wanted for him.

What had happened to him when he went away that changed him so intensely?

Would she, a part of his past, fit into his new world and his future or was this marriage a doomed experiment?

Taking a step back Lilith broke the kiss. She reached up to touch his face and offered him a smile which he immediately returned.

"We should tell your father, or you should. I do not think he will take kindly to my being present for that conversation and I need to take Elaine to our room for her afternoon lessons."

"The man will not be alive in a fortnight. His opinion of my life no longer matters. I am not doing this to spite him I asked you because I cannot think of anyone else that I would like to have beside me for the rest of my life." He grinned and kissed the back of her hand. "At Redbourne, Liam's wife, Caelia sometimes trains with us. She has a sword of her own and is becoming quite the warrior. Would you like that? A sword of your own?"

Lilith smiled in delight. How did he know that she had wanted a sword? Ever since they were youths together she had wondered if she could be proficient with the weapon. To hear that the lady of Redbourne was training with the knights was incredible and made Lilith all the more excited to go with him and start a new life in, what seemed like, a whole new world.

"As long as you are not afraid that I will best you in a duel I would love to learn and for Elaine to learn as well." She turned to take her daughter by the hand. "I will see you at supper. I hope that Moira does not allow her upset to cause a scene. I know that she was expecting to be chosen."

Lionel shook his head and flashed Lilith a smile that made her breath catch in her chest.

"There was never a chance that it would be her, not as long as I was able to make the choice. I could never, ever, live the life that she wants, and it would not be fair to either of us to enter into a union that was doomed to misery and falsehood."

"Thank you, Lionel." She said, letting the breath that she had been holding.

She could not tell him how much it meant to her that she was not a last choice, or one made out of spite. How long had she prayed for a good man to declare his desire to make a life with her? How long had she waited for someone who wanted to make a family with her and Elaine?

So many men that had shown interest either left when they found out about Elaine or they wanted her to send her daughter to the nuns that served the new church opposite to the priests. She would never do such a thing and the fact that they had even suggested it told her everything that she needed to know about them. They were not the kind of man that she wanted or deserved.

Lionel was different.

Lilith was amazed at how he could switch from a gentle, fatherly man with Elaine into the passionate, sensual man she had kissed in the stairway. The carnal longing that she felt when he held her close was wild and untamed. They would wait of course, until the wedding, but when she felt his hand upon her there was little in the world that could hold back her desire to know him physically before he gained the title of husband. Lionel lit a fire in her that she forgot she was capable of feeling. She had never expected that, of all the men in the world, bookish Lionel would turn out to be the man who made her feel like this but ever since he had returned she had not been able to stop thinking about him in ways that she never had before.

Now he was going to be her husband.

The day after tomorrow she would be a wedded woman and Elaine would have the safety and security of a father. There were so many things, so many paths, that would be open to her now and for Lilith as well.

"Mama? What is making you smile like that?" Elaine asked when they arrived in their rooms. "What did Sir Lionel say to you that is making you so happy?"

"Well, sweetheart." She began gently. "Sir Lionel is a good man and an old friend of mine. He has asked me an important question several times today. After seeing how he was treating you and how he defended us against those priests, I made the decision to say yes to his question."

"What was the question and why does it make you happy?" Elaine asked, getting her slate and her chalk for her lessons.

"He asked me to marry him, and I said yes. That makes me happy because after the wedding on Sunday we will be a family with him."

"Forever?"

"Yes, Elaine, forever."

***

"This will destroy the family line forever." Sir Alex bellowed. "You are not marrying that girl. I forbid it."

"You can try, father." Lionel said, forcing himself to be calm. "I am going to marry her on Sunday. If you try to forbid it then I shall wait for Prince Banning to arrive and overrule you. Lilith will be my wife, with or without your approval."

"You are doing this, choosing her, purely to spite me and make a mockery of my command." The old man coughed.

Lionel could not tell if his father's face was red from anger or from the strain of the cough, but it was not going to change his mind.

"That is merely a fringe benefit, father. If you are going to force me to do something I do not want to do you are going to have to accept that I am going do it my way and not yours." Lionel calmly took a sip of wine and smiled. "I want to marry Lilith and I will do so."

"You must swear to me that your children will stand as heirs to what I have done here. I do not want..."

"Do not want what? Do not want any child not your blood to inherit this place? Is it really more valuable to you than the happiness of your children? Why are we, Fiona, and I, never the ones that are important to you? It is always this place that matters, not us." Lionel said in reply.

He was calm on the outside, or trying to be, but inside he was ready to erupt with the mix of disgust and anger he felt at the words. Nothing and no one had ever been or would ever be more important to his father than the stone and mortar of Scotsbane. For a brief moment he wanted to let the priests have it and be done with the whole thing. The only thing that stopped him was knowing that the people needed to be looked after in ways that those priests never would understand.

"This is my responsibility. Uther gave it to me long before Arthur was even born." Alex said, catching his breath and glaring at his son.

Lionel understood responsibility, it had been hammered into his head for as long as he could remember. This was different though. This was his marriage and the event that so much future happiness hinged on. Not only his own now but that of Lilith and Elaine, not to mention Fiona.

"That responsibility is mine now, as are the people. All you need worry about now is preparing to meet your maker."

He did not add the next thought on his mind which was that his father might be wise to use his final days to make amends with those he wronged instead of leaving nothing but bitter memories behind as his legacy. There was nothing left to say between them on the subject, not anymore.

"You can go to the afterlife safe in the knowledge that I will marry and have children, if my wife is as warm to the idea as I am and that Fiona will marry a good man of her own choosing. We will both live out our lives happily with the freedom of choice before us. When you go I want you to know that. We are going to be happy in the future."

"You are an even greater disappointment now than you were when you left." Sir Alex growled. "I thought that going to Camelot, squiring, and becoming a knight, might teach you how to be a man. That you might learn responsibility and how to make sacrifices. Instead you come back weaker. I should have sent you to the monastery instead, at least then you would be out of my way. Your sister knows her place at least. If you go through with this wedding to Lilith I will sign the betrothal document that gives her to Baxter. He can have her whenever he chooses to take her from this house."

"Leave her out of this. I am tired of you hurting her, so she will be coming with me and Lilith after the wedding." Lionel said.

All his life Lionel had wanted to silence his father. To stop the tirade of abuse that poured from his mouth every time that either of his children did something that disappointed or annoyed him. Today the urge was stronger than ever. It was only his fragile health that was stopping Lionel from pinning the old man to the wall and silencing him with his fists.

"You have no power over us anymore. Once I marry Lilith and have Prince Banning ensure that the legal papers are in order you will be as useless as you claim I am and have less power than the daughter you seek to subjugate in a forced marriage. You are done."

Lionel did not wait for his father to say anything, he turned and left the room. There might come a day when he wished that he said something more, perhaps something warm and loving but he did not have it in him, not anymore. The man had tried to control his life for the last time and, even then, it was not good enough. His choice was not good enough. He was not good enough.

Paternity be damned. Lionel was finished living his life in the attempt to please or meet the expectations of other people, especially those who had no knowledge of who he was or what he stood for. From today onward he was going to dedicate his attention, his life, to making sure that his new wife and daughter, as well as any children they added to their family, never had to wonder how he felt about them. They would always know that he cared about them more than a pile of stone and a sword.

There were two bridges left to cross before he could take his new family and go home. He had to wait for the passing of his father, and he had to tell Moira that she was not the one chosen by him, despite the blessing of his father. He had come here prepared for the death of his father, as much as one could be, but telling a woman that she had planned a wedding that would not happen was something he had no idea how to do, at least without breaking her heart.

Chapter 18

Lionel was trying to think of what he was going to say to Moira when he saw her, how he was going to do what he could to let her down easy so that any hurt was lessened and there was no insult given where it was not intended. He could not brush her off as he had other women in the past. She was a friend and his first lover, not some barmaid that he bent over a table to help him sleep on a lonely night.

She may not be a princess or lady of the court and she might be the most sexually forward woman he had ever met, but she was still a woman who deserved respect and kindness from him. He had to treat this with some sensitivity and delicacy. Perhaps offer to let her come with them as far as Camelot and encourage her to meet a man in the city? He was so busy trying to think of ways to make his rejection easier on Moira that he did not see her standing in front of him until he bumped into her.

"My apologies. I did not see you." Lionel said, feeling like an awkward teenager again under the stare that he realized was already full of rage. "I did not hurt you did I? Just now?"

"Hurt? Not in body but in spirit. How could you Lionel? How could you do this to me?" Moira cried.

The way her tightly clenched fists were propped on her hips reminded him of an angry nursemaid and he fought back a smirk.

"Um, what is it exactly that I have done? I have not seen you since this morning so it cannot be anything that I have said."

"Oh, you said it, just not to me." She snapped, her tone suggesting that he should know exactly what she was talking about. "You told Father Ignatius to cancel all my plans for the wedding and said something about it not being my wedding to plan. Why would you do that? Why would you say something so embarrassing to the priest that is going to conduct our ceremony?"

"Our ceremony?" Lionel coughed. "Moira I did not ask for you hand in marriage. I asked Lilith. She and I will be married by a druid, then we will have a basic service in the church to appease the priests and my father."

"Lilith? You cannot be serious." Moira laughed. "She has a child from another man, and you are going to marry her, make her mistress of Scotsbane? How can you? She is completely..."

"She is completely perfect for my vision of my life in the future. She is who I want to be with and is who I will be with." Lionel said firmly. "I am sorry if you thought otherwise, but I have not given you any indication that I wanted to pursue that with you. You did that to yourself."

"Your father gave our union his blessing. He chose me." She was yelling now, and the sound was echoing down the hall.

"I did not choose you." Lionel replied, doing his best not to raise his voice. "It is my life and my marriage. Soon this property will be mine. I will be in command here and Lilith will be at my side as my wife and Elaine will be my daughter, along with any others we will have together. Accept it."

"I had you first. You owe me this by the laws of the church." Moira hissed. "I will not accept this, and I will not accept her. This is my chance to change stations in life, not hers."

Her hands crept up his arms and across his chest. The attempt at seduction was obvious and the part of him that was not disgusted felt bad for her. She thought that this was how she could get a man to love her? There was so much more to her than this and yet she was reducing herself merely to sex.

"I do not follow the new religion Moira. You know that." Lionel said, pulling her hands off of his belt. "We also both know that while you might have been my first that I was not yours, so that clause or rule or divine order does not apply to me and what happened between us."

"You will have to. This is not a choice Lionel. You must." She was nearly shrieking now. "I will talk to the priests, to your father. If they do not do something then I will deal with Lilith myself."

That was something that could not happen. He could deal with the priests, if they dared set foot in this house and he had just dealt with his father. He could do it again if he needed to. If Moira spoke to Lilith there was no telling what lies she would share or how she would twist the truth, which would be worse than the lies. He would have to admit to the true parts and try to convince her that the rest was lies. It would be nearly impossible and, even if he did, she would never forget what Moira said. The attack would haunt his marriage if he let it happen.

"Moira, if you say a word to Lilith that causes strife or stress then I will tell everyone the things I know about your past, including the part regarding me. I do not want to do that. I do not want to hurt you. I have never wanted to hurt you, but if you hurt Lilith and Elaine I will do everything that I can to destroy you."

He watched his words sink in for Moira. She was realizing that he meant every word and that his would carry more weight socially than hers ever could. Even though he would never say an ill word about her under normal circumstances there was no doubt that any attack on his bride and her daughter would bring out his darkest side. He might be knight and therefore a gentleman, but he was a protector above all else.

He would protect his women, even if it were against another woman.

"Do you understand me Moira? Do not try to force me into a fight that you cannot win. I will show no mercy and you will regret it for the rest of your life." Lionel growled, leaning over her. "Do not do this. Let it go."

Moira glared at Lionel with a seething rage smouldering in her dark eyes, but she nodded her compliance. She did not need to like him or respect him at all as long as she feared him enough to leave Lilith alone. This would only last a few days, perhaps weeks if his father's health lasted that long. Then they would all be able to move with their lives. He would be in Redbourne with his new family and his sister while Moira carried on with her life.

No. She could not carry on with her life as it was before. She lived here at Scotsbane and took care of his father. Without Sir Alex she had no livelihood and no prospects for another similar position. Perhaps it would ease the sting a little if he were to offer her some assistance.

"Moira." He held up a finger. "What if you traveled with us as far as Camelot? I am sure the city would hold any number of opportunities for you. You would likely find a better match there than here in Scotsbane, myself included."

He watched her weigh the options and the truth of his words. She could hardly find fault in his offer and he hoped that she would agree to come, even if it were to follow after them.

"You do not want to marry me, but you want me to come with you when you leave here?" She asked, arching a brow at him. "You want to take me to Camelot and see me installed safely in the city?"

There was something in her tone that was beginning to make him uncomfortable, but she was no longer making threats against Lilith or his impending marriage, so he simply nodded.

"Of course. I do not want anything to happen to you. I want you to be as happy as I am going to be." Lionel smiled at her. "Why not think about it and give me your answer after supper. I have to go speak to the groundskeeper and the man who has been helping to manage the estate since my father became ill. The people of Scotsbane must know that they will be protected and that their lives will go on as normal, even after my father is gone."

She gave him a slight nod and a small smile in return.

"Good. Just think about it, a future in Camelot." Lionel said then turned to walk away pleased that the situation that could have been explosive had been mended so simply.

This might not be so hard to carry off, especially after Gerard, Saffir and the royal twins of Gore returned. After they arrived all of this would be bearable. He could introduce his wife to his brothers, and they would all become friends. It would get even better once they returned to Redbourne. When Liam and Caelia got to meet her, they could all start their families together. It would be better than a daydream or fantasy, it would be real life.

The meeting with the groundskeeper and his staff went better than he expected. The man was not only reasonable but thrilled at the prospect of being able to run the estate using some of the newest techniques. It seemed that it was not only his children that Sir Alex stifled with his need to be the only authority.

Lionel hoped that the authority that he was granting the man would keep the property safe from the monastery and the ambitions of the priests. The people here, those that he knew as a child and those who had come to Scotsbane later, deserved to be safe, to be able to live their lives in peace. He wanted for them the same thing that he wanted for himself, happiness or at least a fair chance at it.

By the time that the meeting was done, the men and his workers were full of ideas and eager to share them with someone who would listen, Lionel had just enough time to wash and prepare himself for supper. He felt as nervous as a schoolboy once again when he realized that he would be escorting Lilith to the table under the eyes of both his father and Moira. Neither of them was likely to make the meal pleasant, but he hoped that Lilith was strong enough to deal with the jealousy and disappointment without being threatened. Once he made a decision Lionel stood by it, which meant that he would stand by her no matter what.

When he knocked on her door he was floored by the elegant woman who answered. Lilith was wearing a gown of deep, dark, green and her hair was pulled back from her face with only a few strands curled to frame her delicate features and make the freckles sprinkled across her nose and cheeks stand out beautifully. He could not say for sure, but it looked as though she had accented her eyes and lips with a touch of color. Regardless of what she had done she looked like a goddess of the harvest, her curves round and ripe. His hands ached to caress her, to memorize her body and kiss each freckle as though they were the path to her heart.

"Good evening, Lionel. Fiona was so thrilled by the news when I told her that she insisted that I borrow one of her gowns for dinner tonight." Lilith said with a smile that bordered on shy. "She thought it would help me look the part of a lady. I hope you do not mind?"

"Lilith, you look wonderful. I will have to thank Fiona for her thoughtfulness." Lionel said, trying not to stare. "Though the finery is not needed I cannot deny the difference it makes. You could easily be mistaken for a princess."

He loved that his compliment made her blush. She needed to do that more and he would enjoy making it a part of their day, every day. There was so much to look forward to, so much to learn about her and to share about himself. He wondered, as they walked towards the dining hall, what he would learn about her tomorrow? And the day after that? Would he ever stop being curious about his wife?

"Thank you. I do not think I could pass for one in conversation. My manners would not likely stand up to the criticism of the court, but it is fun to look the part." Lilith said, smiling as they entered the hall and faced the irritated faces of Sir Alex and Moira.

"Though I think, at this moment, I might prefer to be invisible. I am guessing that neither of them took your news as well as you had hoped?" She whispered nervously they approached the table.

"They did not take our news well." Lionel whispered back, emphasizing that they were together in this. "I took care of it though. You are going to be my wife and they will have to accept this. I gave them no choice because you are my choice."

Chapter 19

The dining room had never felt so cold as it did that night.

Lilith had suspected that Sir Alex and Moira would both be displeased that Lionel had chosen her against the old knight's wishes, but she was surprised at the animosity she felt in the air. Moira would not even look at her and Sir Alex would not stop. She was waiting for the moment that he would speak. Even though it would be awful and hurtful it would at least break the silence.

"How are you feeling tonight, Sir Alex?" She finally ventured once the meal was served and there were only the five of them left in the room.

"Like a man who is about to die and leave no worthy legacy behind him." He said in a flat tone that belied the anger in his eyes. "I imagine you are quite pleased with yourself, with your catch."

"My catch?" She said, putting down her cutlery to meet his eyes. "I was not the one who was fishing for a marriage, Sir. All I wanted was to leave Scotsbane with Fiona so that I could start over with a new life."

"You have been angling to trap my son for years. Admit it."

"Father, you have no right to say such things." Lionel cut in.

"Lionel, thank you, but I can defend myself on this topic." Lilith said, resting her hand on her future husband's forearm. "I have nothing to hide from anyone."

"Is that so?" Moira said, joining the conversation from beside a visibly distressed Fiona. "You, of all people at this table, have nothing to hide? I think you are lying to yourself Lilith as well as Lionel."

"I am not the one who tried to trap him, Moira, and I am not the one who tried to blackmail him into a marriage he did not want." Lilith said calmly, her hands planted firmly on the surface of the table so that no one could see them tremble with emotion. "Which of us had already spoken to priests in a religion Lionel does not follow to start planning a wedding before they were proposed to? I do not think that was me."

"How dare you say such a thing." Moira said, dropping her knife to the table. "You, with a bastard child out of wedlock, would judge me for planning ahead based on the word of Sir Alex that this would happen?"

"Moira! If you use that word again I will have to rethink our words in the corridor." Lionel said, his tone as dark and foreboding as the look that was on Sir Alex's face. "I will not stand for such talk."

"She can say what she likes. This is still my house Lionel." Sir Alex said.

Fiona looked at Moira then at Lilith with a horrified expression.

"Moira, you told me that you were talking to the priests to tell them that I did not want to marry Sir Baxter, no matter what happened. You lied to me? You would have let them force me into that marriage, not knowing that it was against my wishes? I trusted you to help me."

"I had to choose who to help and I needed it more. I could do more to help you as your sister-in-law than I could having a conversation with the priests." Moira shrugged. "It seemed the best course of action since you did not care enough to talk to them yourself."

"Because I was trying to keep it secret. That is no longer necessary now that Lionel is marrying Lilith, which you should both know that I fully support even if you do not." Fiona said to Sir Alex and Moira. "Not because I was afraid."

The smile that Fiona offered made Lilith feel as though she had another ally in the fight against Moira, whom she never thought was a close friend, but certainly had never considered to be her enemy. With Lionel and Fiona backing her, supporting her, Lilith was certain that there was nothing that Moira and Sir Alex could do to ruin this now.

"You thought that my priests would listen to your wishes over my command? You must be thicker in the head than I thought." Alex sneered at his daughter. "Whoever thought that the word of women would carry weight in the world of men should have their head examined."

"Father, I think that you are losing yourself." Lionel said, with an awkward flush rising up his neck when he turned to look at Lilith. "I swear that is not how I think. I respect your mind. I respect you."

Lilith smiled at him and took his hand in hers but before she could say anything to thank him for his sweet words his father spoke again to further embarrass his son.

"So now both my children flout my orders, my teachings and everything I have ever held dear. I should have just let you stay in the south and let the church take over here before you even knew I was gone. I have never been so disappointed with you, both of you, as I am right now." Sir Alex slowly rose to his feet and began to shuffle towards the door. "Let that be my legacy then. I have spawned not one but two useless children who will hold back the progression of society because they are clinging to the past. I would wish your marriages good luck but even that seems impossible for you two."

Lilith watched both Fiona and Lionel flinch as if they had been physically struck. How many times before had such words come with a heavy hand when they were younger and unable to defend themselves? How many things were able to be explained about both of them with this knowledge? She gave Lionel's hand a light squeeze and smiled kindly at her dear, damaged, knight. To let him know that she was there to support him.

When she looked across the table to give a reassuring look to Fiona she saw Moira's expression, smug and triumphant. How could a woman that revelled in the pain of those around her have thought that she would be the one to marry such a compassionate man? She was not even pretending to care that Fiona was hurting. After years in this house, helping to dress her, and sharing the intimacies that all young women did at their age Moira was acting as though there was nothing at all between them.

How could she be so cruel? So heartless?

When the door closed behind Sir Alex the four of them finished their meal in silence. Moira gloating, Fiona, and Lionel with an air of dejection and sorrow, while Lilith's mind was whirling with possibilities of how she could make this a little better for the siblings. She was still wondering what she could do as Lionel walked her and Fiona back to their respective rooms, pointedly leaving Moira to walk alone.

When they reached Fiona's room Lilith took a few steps away, after giving her future sister a warm embrace for comfort. She wanted to give the siblings some privacy to say whatever they needed to while they held each other tight. Her heart hurt for them both. Though she may have lost both her parents while she had them they were wonderful and loving towards her. She cannot imagine how different her life would be if she had a parent like Sir Alex.

When Lionel rejoined her for the next stage of their stroll Lilith took his arm and let her head rest on his shoulder.

"I am sorry for how awful your father was tonight. I did not know he was like that with the two of you. It must hurt." She said softly.

"Yes and no. It used to hurt a lot more, but now it is more a memory of the pain of the past that is not fully healed. Fiona still hopes to win his approval. I learned long ago that I never would." Lionel said,

His voice was calm, but Lilith could not help but wonder how much hurt was still hidden beneath that pain.

"Is there anything that I can do to ease it? Even old wounds ache sometimes, and I would like to help if I can." She asked, stopping to look up into his beautiful, but sad, blue eyes. "Let me help you, husband."

She said the word just to try the sound of it, which she liked more than she thought she would.

He shook his head and said. "Make that word true in every sense of the word and I will be the happiest man in Briton. Soon enough we will have our ceremony and forge an unbreakable bond. That will make me happy Lilith." He raised her hand to his lips and placed a soft kiss to her palm. "Goodnight, rest well. I will see you in the morning, wife."

"Goodnight, husband." She said with a smile.

Stepping into her room and closing the door behind her, Lilith walked slowly to the door of the bedroom and peeked inside to make sure that Elaine was fast asleep. She quickly changed out of the beautiful borrowed gown and into one of her own dresses. She tugged on her boots and wrapped a dark, warm, cloak around her shoulders. She knew what she wanted to do, what would make Lionel smile a little brighter, and she was going to do it right now.

Moira would likely have snuck into his bedroom, again, to use her body to ease the pain that Lionel was feeling, if she noticed it at all. Lilith would do that too, another night, when they were married but this was something even better than that. It would be a much more permanent solution than just going to bed with her husband. She was going to find a druid to come to Scotsbane tomorrow and perform the traditional wedding ceremony for them before they performed the one in the church to satisfy his father and the law. The smile it would put on Lionel's face would be wonderful. She hoped that her action would show to him that she was committed to their union as much as he was. That she wanted this too.

A small lantern from the kitchen and a word with the guard at the gate were all she needed before stepping out into the dark of the forest. She was looking for the hut of the local druid. It had been some time since she had been to see him, but she knew the old man well. He would be proud, thrilled, to perform such a ceremony for the new lord of Scotsbane. This was not something to be taken lightly.

The woods were calm and still, the moon was high in the sky and there were almost no sounds from animals. She was not lost. She knew the woods too well for that, even in the dark. There was something, a feeling, telling her to stop and wait where she was. He would come to her. This was his place.

"You have been away a long-time child. What brings you to me in the dark of night?" The deep voice she knew so well spoke from the shadows. "There were no portents of illness or death."

"This is a celebration, wise one." She said with a bow and a smile. "The new lord of Scotsbane is returned and he is still of the old faith."

"This pleases you, child? That he is returned to us and keeps the faith?" He asked. "Why?"

"It pleases because he has asked for me to marry him and he wishes for a true ceremony. Will you come to the garden?" She asked, unable to hide her happiness and her hope.

"I cannot." He said, stepping out of the shadows. "Those vows should not be said behind a wall, but over free water surrounded by nothing except the spirits of the old ones."

"What would you have me do? This blessing is important to him and to me." She asked. It would be difficult to surprise Lionel if the instructions were too complicated. He would want to stay close to Scotsbane in case his father's health faded quickly.

"It will be good for the land and the people who live upon it." The druid said. "I will perform the ceremony in the north field at the height of noon. The people from the village and our people can bear witness to their new Lord choosing the old religion, their religion. This is what we needed."

Lilith smile and bowed respectfully to the druid as he stepped backwards into the treeline.

"I will make it so and will greet you with joy when the sun is at it's peak. Thank you, wise one, for all that you do for us."

It was only a moment later, but she knew that she was alone again. Her plan for the surprise for Lionel was going to be everything she hoped for. Fiona would likely help her to get ready in something simple as well as in getting Lionel out of Scotsbane and into the field to meet the druid.

Tomorrow night, if all went as planned, she would be his wife in the eyes of the gods and the people. His wife.

Chapter 20

The next morning was as tense and awkward for Lionel as the previous evening had been. Moira was glaring at him whenever their paths crossed, and his father was staying to his bedchambers. He wondered if that was due to anger or if it was his health? It might be a good idea to check in on him later that afternoon, just in case it was serious. He would not put it past the old man to fake a decrease in his health simply to cause strain and stress for his children.

He had barely had a chance to speak to Lilith that morning, the groundskeeper had wanted to continue with the planning for the estate in the future. The few times that Lionel had seen her, from a window or across a room she had flashed him a smile. It was reassuring that she was so happy even after the night before. The mess that his father and Moira cultivated over the table could have been much worse.

For Fiona it had been. The last time Lionel had seen her that upset over things their father had said was the night before he had left for Camelot. He had held her while she cried that night and last night he had wanted to do the same. She was stronger now, from age or becoming used to their father's vicious tongue being directed at her was not clear, but he still wanted to keep her safe from harm.

The concern for his own well being that Lilith had shown was more comforting than he had expected it to be. He had gone to sleep dreaming of being held in her arms, not in the throws of passion, but simply taking comfort in the calmness of her presence, in her soothing touch. He had never allowed himself such a luxury before, and now it was his most relaxing thought before he went to sleep. He would never tell her that Moira had been waiting at his door, in nothing more than her linen shift nightdress. It was clear what she wanted. Despite their earlier conversation and the way that she had spoken at the dining table, the woman still thought that he would welcome her to his bed? She had to be outside her mind or think that he was a fool to fall for such an obvious trap.

He had dismissed her without even bothering to look at her. With a simple goodnight, slam of his door and a deliberate locking of his door, as well as the secret entrances, he had ensured that his point was made as well as his honor intact. There was a definite concern that she would make another attempt that night or cause a scene at the church ceremony in the morning. He could hardly deny her attendance on a hunch, but he would certainly task a guardsman with making sure that she did not get a chance to do anything that would ruin the day for Lilith. His woman deserved every happiness that he could give her.

Lionel was sitting at his father's desk, soon to be his, and reading over some of the reports on field productivity when the very woman upon his mind appeared at the door.

"Lilith? What brings you here? Not that I mind the distraction, it is simply unexpected." He said with a smile so broad his face hurt. "Can I do something for you?"

"Actually, I think that there is something that I can do for you." She said, gliding into the room like magic. "Have you eaten?"

"Yes." He cocked his head to the side. "One of the girls brought me a plate. I hope you were not planning a picnic."

"No. Not a picnic, something better than that." She beamed at him and held out her hand. "Come with me. I have a wonderful surprise for you."

"I am intrigued. Is it not still the custom for wedding gifts to be presented on the wedding day? I suppose early is not a bad thing, but yours from me is not ready yet." Lionel said, standing and taking her by the hand.

"It is a gift, but not of the kind that you think. Come and see." Lilith said urgently.

He was surprised at how much excitement he felt, how infectious her enthusiasm was. Rushing through the hallways felt like child's play and he half expected to exit into the garden to find some adult adaptation of a game arranged for them to play together. It was surprising when Lilith led the way towards the gate on the Northern wall of the property. Perhaps it was the villagers wishing to offer a congratulatory cheer to the couple, which would be warmer and more heartfelt than his father would have ever been able to muster, even before he got sick.

"Where are we going?" Lionel asked when they reached the edge of the field.

He looked around, noticing that there were many more workers in the field than normal. Had there been something in the meeting with the groundskeeper that he had missed or not understood?

"We are going to see the druid. He will marry us today, before the farce in the church occurs instead of after. It is a gift, from me to you." Lilith said, adjusting her dress and pointing to the small cluster of people near the tree at the center of the field. "Fiona and Elaine are there waiting. This puts your desire for a traditional ceremony, the old ceremony, before the wish and command of your father."

He was shocked. In awe that she had thought of this and arranged it before he even knew how such a thing would make him feel. For the first time his wishes overruled those of his father, instead of simply being permitted after the command of the old man had already been followed. No matter what anyone did or said, protested or claimed, after this they would be married. A lawful husband and wife.

"You arranged our wedding?" He turned to look at her. "Lilith this is wonderful. I never would have thought of this. Thank you."

"You are most welcome. I wanted to do something to cheer you up after last night and I know that you like to do things that defy your father, on a technical point if not blatantly." Lilith said walking towards the tree with him. "This was the most defiant thing that I could think of. I went out last night to find the druid to ask him to agree to do the service."

"Wait." He stopped and turned her to look at him. "You went out into the forest by yourself last night? At that late hour? Lilith you cannot do that. It is dangerous."

"Lionel, I have lived here my whole life. I know those wood better than you do." Lilith shook her head. "I was perfectly safe. You do not need to worry."

"I will always worry about you Lilith. That is part of my job as a husband. I hope that you will worry about me too?" He cupped her chin in his hand and raised her eyes to meet his. "We look out for each other, always. Even if it seems like a small worry or something simple, we will take care of each other and do what we can to make each other safe. Agreed?"

"Agreed." She said softly. "And we will both do the same for Elaine."

"Yes. Of course, Elaine and any other children that we might have together."

Lionel watched the pain and emotion filling Lilith's eyes. Had no one ever told her that before? Made a promise to take care of her? To care about her? He was going to take a special pleasure in showing her that a man can keep his word to a woman. It might take years, but every time he made a promise and kept it the pain would be less and less until it was gone completely.

He was going to love being married to her and showing her what a good man was.

They continued their walk to the tree, holding each other by the hand with smiles on both their faces. It was such a simple, beautiful, moment as they stepped through the wheat and yet he felt like a king with a great queen at his side. The whole world, his life, hers, and Elaine's would never be the same. This was a new beginning.

Lionel gave a small nod to Fiona, but it was the druid that stopped him in his tracks. The old man turned from the alter to face the betrothed couple and it was not the same man from his childhood. This was Merlin from the court in Camelot.

Lionel dropped to a knee and bowed his head.

"Lord Merlin, this honor is beyond my station. Thank you for this great gift."

"Lionel, young lord of Redbourne, the honor is mine to be present and able to perform something so intimate and innocent as a wedding in the old ways. There are few now who would request such a thing over the more elegant church affairs."

"I admit that it was not my idea. I never would have intruded upon you for such a thing, but I will stand eternally grateful that the woman I am about to marry was bold enough to do so." Lionel squeezed Lilith's hand.

"Then, if you will both stand, we shall begin." Merlin said, bringing Lionel to his feet.

He still could not believe that this was happening. A quick glance at Lilith told him that she knew, or at least suspected how excited having Merlin himself perform the ceremony would make him. What a deviously cleaver woman she was.

As Merlin bound their wrists and hands with a cord Lionel stared down into Lilith's dark eyes. He felt a peace that he had not expected. Everything was right now.

The calm, deep voice of the druid began to recite the words of the ancient ceremony.

"Let there be peace in the East, so let it be. Let there be peace in the South, so let it be. Let there be peace in the West, so let it be. Let there be peace in the North, so let it be. Let there be peace through all the Worlds. So, let it be."

He looked at the townsfolk that were gathered around the tree, watching the ceremony with the same eagerness as they would have for a beloved son and daughter.

"Lilith and Lionel. As our Circle is woven and consecrated, this moment in time and this place become blessed. Let each soul truly be here that the spirits of those gathered may be blended in one sacred space, with one purpose and one voice. All things in nature are circular. Night becomes day, day leads into night which again gives way today. Moon waxes and wanes, and waxes again. There is Spring, Summer, Autumn and Winter, then Spring returns again. These are the flowing rhythms of the Cycle of Existence. Yet in the Centre of the Circle is the stillness of the Source, eternal and brilliant."

Merlin looked first at Lilith and then to Lionel.

"Lilith and Lionel, do you bring with you this day your symbols of these mysteries of life?"

Lionel realized that they had nothing for rings or offerings. If he had known it would have been easy to arrange but the surprise left him unprepared. He sighed with relief when Fiona stepped close and held up a small bag.

"We do." Lionel and Lilith answered the druid.

Fiona withdrew rings and delivered them to be blessed. How many bridegrooms were left wondering what their wedding bands looked like at their ceremony? There had likely never been a wedding like this before.

"Let them then be blessed in the name of the old gods of our land, for they are an outward sign and a sacred reminder of your commitment witnessed here this day."

The rings were then blessed, consecrated, and placed upon the altar. Lionel still could not see which rings they were and wondered if Lilith had chosen them or Fiona. It would not surprise him if it had been his little sister. She knew where all the family treasures were hidden.

"As the sun and moon bring light to the Earth, do you, Lilith and Lionel, vow to bring the light of love and joy to this union?"

"I do." Lilith said, smiling up at him.

"I do." Lionel said, stroking her finger with his own.

The druid held out his hand with the rings resting in his palm. Lilith picked up a thick gold band with a dark blue stone embedded in the top and slid it onto his finger with a smile. The one that he picked up, that Fiona had chosen to Lilith, had a large, rectangle cut sapphire that was flanked by small diamonds at the top of the band. It was the perfect pair of rings for them.

"Do you vow to honor each other as you honor that which you hold sacred above all things?"

"I do." They both replied.

"Then with my blessing and that of the old gods and the new, I pronounce that you be husband and wife from this day forward. Let no man or woman break asunder what has been joined here in divinity. You seal your union with a kiss." Merlin said, with a broad grin as he lifted his hands and the people raised their voices in celebration.

Lionel pulled Lilith tight to his chest. Their still bound hands pressed between them as he lowered his lips to hers and took her mouth in a kiss of passionate possession. Their tongues colliding, tasting each other. It was explosive. Full of desire and utterly lacking in the chastity he had expected from her.

"Hello wife." He said when they broke the kiss to take a breath.

Chapter 21

"Hello husband." Lilith said with more joy in her heart than she had ever expected to feel when she got married. She had expected a feeling of resignation, perhaps contentment, not this shiver of excitement and anticipation.

Lionel's reaction to the high druid performing the marriage rights was charming. She knew that he respected the druid but had no idea how much. It made him seem a little more human and approachable to know that, just like anyone else, Lionel had personal heroes.

They walked to the edge of the field with their hands still tied together. Traditionally they would have stayed bound until they went to bed that night, but they both had work to do and it would be best if the ceremony were kept a secret from Moira and Sir Alex for the moment. The secrecy was not due to shame or guilt. Instead it came from a desire to keep the bliss of the moment, the knowledge that they were married before the eyes of their gods, a private piece of joy for as long as possible. There was no good that would come from bragging to the others of what was done, and it would cause strife where it was not needed.

"I must return to my work, and I am certain that you must have a few things that you wish to see to this afternoon." Lionel said while Fiona unbound their wrists and handed the cord to Lilith.

"In case you want to hit him with it later for, inevitably, being an ass."

Lionel hugged his little sister with a warm smile and kissed her cheek.

"Wait until it is your turn to marry. The advice I will have for him so that he can deal with you will fill a tome."

"Thank you Fiona." Lilith said with a laugh. "I will keep that in mind. For now, I think that I would like to go and prepare a room for our wedding night.

"That is a wonderful, thoughtful thing to do. Thank you Lilith." Lionel said in what she was starting to think of as his 'Lord of the Manner' tone. He seemed to use it when his emotions were high, and he was trying to remain calm. It was something worth noting about her new husband.

"I will see you tonight, at dinner, then. Will you tell your father?" Lilith said, still holding his hand.

"I see no reason to start another fight with him in his last days. This was for us not for them." He said before he kissed the back of her hand. "Now I will go and get everything done for the day so that we may enjoy the night and what tomorrow brings."

She watched him walk away and sighed. What a man.

Lilith spent the rest of the day preparing one of the grandest rooms in the guest wing for their wedding night. She set candles around the room as well as flowers from the garden that Elain helped her pick. She even made a point of finding cedar shavings and heather in the fire stores so that the room would have a wonderful smell through the night. It felt wonderful to do this for him, to take care of him even if it was something small.

She sat on the bed and leaned her head against one of the posts that held up the canopy. It had been years since she had been with a man like this and, though she would never admit it to anyone, the few times that she had been with Elaine's father it had never been in a bed. She could not let Lionel know that though. He knew that she had been with a man before, obviously, but he still thought she was a lady, not a foolish girl who let a man raise her skirts behind the barn.

What was she going to do tonight? Act the part of the demure, nearly virginal bride? Let loose her passion and be the aggressor? What would he like? What would he be expecting from her? Lilith stood and began to pace the floor trying to figure out what she should do, how she should plan this. She wished that Moira were a friend that she could go to with this problem, but there was no chance that she would give good or honest advice on this subject with this man. Not after last night.

It was still on her mind when she sat down at the dining table next to Lionel and across from Fiona. It made her nervous that Sir Alex or Moira might have heard about the ceremony in the field and start another argument that would ruin the joy of the day. It was hard not to smile across the table at the woman who was now her sister, especially each time that Moira spoke with her voice full of mockery and disdain. Lilith wanted to laugh and tell the other woman that she had already lost, but that would not make anything better.

Sitting in absolute silence seemed to work almost as well though, for both Sir Alex and Moira were getting more agitated with every course of the meal. Finally, the plates were cleared, and Sir Alex left the table so they could all depart to their rooms. It felt strange to hold hands with Lionel through the hallway and as they approached the room she had prepared Lilith had to wonder if Lionel was feeling nervous as well. She had asked one of the girls in the kitchen to go ahead of them to light the candles and the fire.

"I hope you like what I have done with the room, Lionel. I really had to guess at what kind of things a man would find romantic, but I think it turned out well."

She opened the door and guided him into the softly lit room. It was even better in the dark than she had thought it would be. She turned to look at Lionel, eager to see what he thought of it and was rewarded for her efforts. His blue eyes were sparkling in the candlelight as he turned around, taking in everything that she had done.

"Lilith, this is amazing. I have never seen a room like this before. It is like something out of a fairy tale or one of those poems that my sister and Caelia, Liam's wife, like to read for the romance. You did all this for me?" Lionel said, reaching for her hand.

"For us." Wrapping her arms around his torso. "I wanted to give us a perfect night, far away from the rest of the house, to enjoy each other."

"Mmhmm. I would like to enjoy you, my wife, right now." He said to her as he lowered his head to take her mouth in a kiss.

Beginning gently, as though he was testing the waters of her reception to the attention, his lips pressed against hers. When Lilith parted her lips with a soft moan Lionel was quick to dart his tongue between them to taste her mouth. His kiss tasted like the rich red wine they had enjoyed with dinner and Lilith wanted to drink him in with a reckless abandon.

Slowly she slid her hands up his chest, feeling every inch of hard muscle beneath his linen shirt and wondering what he would look like bared before her in the dim flickering light. One hand began to tug at the string tightening the neckline of Lionel's shirt while the other threaded into his short, sand-brown hair so that she could pull him closer.

His hands were moving up and down Lilith's back slowly, easing closer to her breasts each time. He was taking it slowly and yet ensured that there was no question about what he was thinking, wanting. The straining fabric of his breeches pressing against her confirmed the desire of her husband in a much more visceral way and Lilith yearned to slide her hand from the tip to the base and back again. She wanted to hear him groan in anticipation and watch his eyes close while her gave in to the physical stimulation of her touch.

She wanted to shower him with pleasure.

Breaking the kiss with a gasp Lilith let Lionel lead her to the chair by the fireplace.

"Let's make ourselves a little more comfortable." He murmured in her ear, then trailed kisses down her neck until his lips met the fabric of her dress.

"Yes, you should have a seat, husband." Lilith said, using both hands to push him backwards into the deep cushion of the chair.

He surprised her when he hooked his hands behind her knees causing her to fall astride his lap. Lilith laughed at his playfulness and reached up to unpin her dark hair. When she leaned down to kiss him again, she started tugging his shirt free from his pants, eager to see and feel his bare chest.

"If you are going to do that then I think we should unlace this gown at the very least." Lionel said, sliding her dress from her shoulders with one hand while the other worked the laces that went up her back. As soon as he completed his mission Lilith felt her breasts fall from the confines of the dress and into his hand.

Sitting upright to pull his shirt off and toss it to the floor beside the chair Lilith was delighted to see how her husband's eyes lit up at the site of her bare astride him. She brought his hands up to cup her breasts, sliding her own down his arms so that she could caress his chiseled muscles, while she rolled her hips to grind against his growing erection.

"Oh, this will not do, wife." Lionel said, his voice deep and strained by desire. "You have too many clothes on.

"What?" She replied, her own voice surprisingly husky. "What do you mean?"

She had never been naked with a man, never undressed with one, even down to her shift. She could not imagine letting him see the stretch marks from her pregnancy or the inches she had not lost but that were held back from sight by clever tricks of dress. He thought she was beautiful in her dress, that would certainly change if he saw her completely nude.

He stood up suddenly, their proximity showing how he towered over her with the power and pure masculinity of an alpha wolf. Quickly, before she could protest, he pulled the gown over her hips to the floor. He caught her wrists in between his fingers while the other hand unfastened and pushed her underclothes aside until they too fell to the floor and she was naked under his gaze.

"My god."

His voice was unlike anything that she had ever heard. Lilith struggled to free her hands so that she could cover the parts of herself that must be horrifying to him.

"Lionel, I..." She stammered in a whisper.

"You are the most beautiful woman I have ever seen Lilith. you look divine. So soft, so warm. It is all I can do to stop myself from touching every inch of you. How can it be true that this goddess is my wife?"

He reached out and ran his fingers down her body, across the softness of her stomach to grab hold of her hip and draw her closer to his body. She could smell him now, leather and musk, and his still clothed erection pressed firmly against her stomach.

"I do not have the firm body that I did before Elaine. I will never have that body again." She tried to explain, a blush burning on her cheeks. "Moira..."

"Moira has the body of stick. A lovely one but still a stick none the less. You have created life and have the divine curves of a goddess. My goddess." He said looking her in the eyes so intently that she could not help but believe him.

Before Lilith could think of anything to answer him with that might be comparable or equally flattering her husband lifted her by her thighs. He wrapped her legs around his waist and walked them both towards the bed while he nipped and teased her nipples into tight buds. Easing her back onto the bed Lionel continued his oral attentions to her breasts, her neck, her mouth, and even her eye lids while his hips thrust and rolled against hers. The friction was intense and reminded her body of things she had forced it to forget, urges she had denied for too long and needs she had ignored.

She needed more and she needed it to be now, with her husband.

Giving into her instincts Lilith rolled over on the big bed until Lionel was beneath her. His hands were caressing her inner thigh when she shifted from straddling his hips to his stomach so that she could reach behind to unlace him.

"Come closer Lilith." He growled, trying to move her legs so that she was nearer to his face. "I want more of you."

"Lionel?" She paused her first stroke of his shaft. What was it that he wanted? He could not possibly want her to do that, could he?

She got her answer when his hands grasped her buttocks and pulled her bodily to his mouth. She had heard of this from other women, but Elaine's father had never done anything more than wet her quim before penetration. The first touch of Lionel's tongue between her folds was a burst of sensation and pleasure unlike anything she had ever known. She cried aloud, arching her back with each stroke. She thought that she would rise right off the bed, but Lionel took hold of her wrists and held her in place, forcing her to take the pleasurable lashing of his tongue.

Chapter 22

Lionel woke up with a smile on his face and his wife in his arms. The night had been wonderful and so much more than he had thought it would be.

He had given Lilith pleasure in ways that she had never experienced before. He still had a hard time believing that she had never been the subject of a man's intent like that before. The man she had been with before him had never spent the time to pleasure her, explore her, and turn her climax into the most important thing.

He had devoured her, lapping at her core until she came apart in shivering spasms of pleasure. Then he had laid her beside him, kissing her mouth, neck, shoulders, and chest while his fingers teased and then plunged deep inside her where his cock longed to be. He brought her, again and again, teasing and tantalizing every nerve filled sensitive spot on her beautiful body until she lay quivering in bliss and exhaustion.

Only then, when she was fully satisfied, did he ask for his own pleasure. She welcomed him between her honey sweet thighs with a breathy gasp as he sank home. They moved together like magic, thrusting, and rolling in a battle of passionate wills where they both stood the victor at the end. The softness of her body that had caused her to blush and try to hide had felt so good beneath him. It was a whole new world of physical delight.

She was as passionate and aggressive as he was. Unlike other women who were passive once they moved beyond kissing and petting Lilith was not afraid to take what she wanted from him. When she mounted his cock and rode him like a stallion at a breakneck pace he had held tight to her hips and marveled at the sexual prowess of the woman he had married.

When they were both sated and exhausted with their efforts Lionel had been surprised that she thought she should put the light cotton shift that lay in a pile before the fire back on instead of sleeping naked beside each other.

"Why would you cover that beautiful body again?" He asked from the bed. "Come back here and lay with me Lilith. I want to feel you next to me and memorize the feel of those curves all through the night."

"Lionel." She said, walking back towards the bed with the fabric in her hands. "You do not want to me bare in the light of day. The morning light will reveal all the flaws that might seem easy to ignore in the candlelight but will be impossible to in the daylight."

"Woman, you will not speak of the beauty that is my wife in such a way ever again." Lionel said, rising from the bed. He took the dress from her hand and threw it back towards the fire. "I have never seen a woman as beautiful as you are, inside and out. Will you let me hold you? Let me feel your heart beating in your chest against my skin? We have made love like a man and wife. Will you give me the chance to start falling in love with you? Will you take that risk with me?"

He had thought she was going to cry, but instead she let him bring her back to the bed and hold her all through the night. He did not tell her that he had never spent a night sleeping in a bed with a woman. One of them had always left so he had always woken up alone. This, waking up with her draped across him, was how he wanted to find himself every morning from now on.

"Good morning husband." Lilith said, breaking his thoughts. "I trust you slept well."

"Good morning, wife." He replied, giving her a gentle kiss to her lips. "I did indeed. Better than ever before. Are you ready to get up and prepare for the church service my father commanded for today?"

"I would rather stay in bed with you than do that. The dress alone is enough to exhaust me." She said with a shy smile, pulling the sheet of the bed up to her neck. "I will be happy to have it finished though, so that no man, woman or priest can invalidate our marriage."

"There is no man or woman who can do that now regardless." Lionel said, kissing her forehead and getting out of the bed. "Gerard and Saffir will be back with the royal twins any day, and things are arranged with the a so that he can run things here without the need for me to stay. Do you think Elaine will be alright moving to Redbourne?"

He knew that Lilith would be happy in the south, that Elaine might not be had just occurred to him. The child was young and surely she was adaptable, but this was the only home she had ever known. She might not like the idea of a new home that more like a house than a castle.

"I think that as long as we are all together she will be happy." Lilith replied as she finished dressing. "Now, we must pretend to be an excited bride and groom eager for the ceremony and all that it brings."

"It will not be hard to do as I am a man excited to be able to shower his wife with affection absent the judgement of others." Lionel said, closing the bedroom door behind them. "I suppose I should leave you here, to avoid the whispers and risk that they might reach the wrong ears before the service."

"Yes." She replied with a nod, stepping close to him. "The next time you see me will be in the church. I look forward to seeing you all dressed up."

"I look forward to the same."

Lionel could not help but laugh before he dropped a kiss on her cheek and headed off towards his room to eat and dress for the service. The smile on his face walking back to the main wing of the house was so broad that it was almost painful. He did not realize how much of a daze he was in until he heard the voice of Saffir.

"Well now. That is the look of a cat that got into the cream if ever I saw one."

"He does look considerably happier than the last time I saw his face in Camelot." The polished voice of Prince Banning replied.

"It must be a girl. Only a girl could make Sir Serious smile like that." Princess Elin chimed in as Lionel approached his door.

Gerard stepped away from the group to extend his hand and whisper in his ear.

"So, you chose Lilith then? Good man. Good choice."

"You knew that was going to happen?" Lionel asked with a grin, shaking his hand, and looking over the blacksmith's shoulder to Saffir and the royals. "Step inside you lot. I am sure that whoever brought you up here will be bringing enough breakfast for all of you in a few moments."

"I knew that it was the right choice." Ger said. "Just hoped that you were smart enough to see it and that we would not have to use royal influence in order to set things right."

"You may still need to do just that." Lionel said ushering them in to his room. "There is likely to be at least one voice raised in protest at the ceremony. Prince Banning, Princess Elin, I am thrilled to have you both here for my wedding ceremony today. I am sure that you will both like my wife, Lilith, and her daughter Elaine very much and enjoy their company on the trip back to Redbourne that I pray is as early as possible."

In any other setting he would have had to be more formal with the twins, they were all good friends though and the fact that he had caught Ger and the Prince kissing in Camelot and revealed the secret to no one, even Liam, had earned him the trust of the royals.

"I simply cannot believe that you are getting married Lionel." Elin said giving the knight a quick embrace and kiss on the cheek. "I remember when I was the girl you could not help but stare at, unable to think of something to say. I will not tell her that though. I brought a dress for her, your bride. As soon as we have eaten and caught up on the delicious drama you referred to then I will go and help Fiona dress her to look the part of a princess for the day."

"Thank you Elin. I am sure that Lilith will appreciate that more than I will ever understand." Lionel said as the servants arrived with enough food for all five of them.

Once they were alone, he started to explain what had happened while they were gone. He told them about the service performed by Merlin the day before and how Moira had threatened to try to force a wedding due to their tryst years ago.

"I do not think that my father has the strength left to cause much of a scene, but Moira is still angry enough to attempt something, especially with the backing and support of those priests. They want access to Scotsbane badly enough to side with her, forget their preaching about sex before marriage and try to force that union. It does not help that they despise Lilith for having a child out of wedlock and refusing to join their order of nuns."

"From what I know of those orders the women are used for slave labour and barely better than concubines for the desires of the priests." Ger said, setting down a piece of bread and looking at Prince Banning.

"True in my experience as well, Ger. It is not only the women that are abused in such a manner. The young initiates are treated in a similar fashion. They are far too powerful already and always seeking more. One day I fear that they will hold more power than the throne." The prince added.

"Then it is a good and noble thing that you have saved Lilith and her daughter from this fate Lionel." Elin said, standing and picking up a bag that she had brought with her.

"I think it is the other way around Elin. She may have saved me, or her daughter saved us both." Lionel said. "If you are going for the dressing then you will find them in Fiona's room. Do you remember the way?"

"I remember it like it was only yesterday when we all use to have adventures together. You boys get things sorted out here while I take care of the bride and your sister." She said slipping out the door and down the hall.

"What do you need us to do? I highly doubt that we can physically do much to Moira if she makes a mess of your ceremony." Saffir said, taking a seat on a windowsill. "I would not mind taking a swing at those priests though."

"I think all of us would like the chance at that Saffir." Ger said. "That option aside, what else can we do?"

"Be ready to stand up and argue that I am already married to Lilith by the laws and faith that we follow. Arthur has not made the new church the official religion of the land and does not require us to follow it's laws yet."

"What about finding Merlin? I doubt the old druid has left the area yet?" Banning suggested. "If Saffir could find him I am certain that I could delay the priests long enough to get him here. They are not brave enough to face him, especially if he feels insulted. That kind of rage would terrify anyone, but especially those with false power."

Lionel was relieved that his friends had arrived in time to help. There was no way that his own protests would be enough to silence the priests. They might be forced to listen to a prince though.

"As quickly as you can Saffir. These priests are firmly set on gaining control of Scotsbane and gods know what other properties. We have to set a precedent against them as well as keep them out of my marriage bed."

"I will be back with Merlin, if he will come, as quickly as I can." Saffir said, heading to the door. "May I borrow one of your horses? Ours are still tired from the ride through the night."

"Take what you need with my blessing. Hurry back. I do not want to risk being stuck married to Moira."

The other knight was laughing as he left. Lionel knew that if anyone could find the druid it was Saffir.

"Alright boy, now that the plan is in place, we should see about getting you dressed. Bathe first though. You do not want to go to the chapel smelling of a wedding night that you do not want the priests to know already happened."

Ger said with a dark grin. "Let us ensure that the only offence brought today is to the priests, not the noses of everyone in the chapel."

Chapter 23

It was a few hours later, though it felt like only moments, when Lionel found himself standing near the alter in the chapel of the new church near Scotsbane. He did not want to be here. He was already married. This was ridiculous and if his father were more reasonable, or sicker, he would not be going through with this. He certainly hated putting Lilith through this farce.

Looking around the room his relief at the timely arrival of his friends was reinforced when he met the angry, disgusted, eyes of his father. This was what he had asked for but because it was not the exact details that he had wanted it was, of course, not good enough. It was so easy to get caught up in the negativity that radiated off his father that Lionel had to mentally fight to avoid the fall. It had obviously happened to Moira. She looked as though she were at either a funeral or a trial.

He had never seen her like that and as much as he did not want to marry her or be around her, Lionel could not help but feel sorry for her disappointment. She had thought that her life was changing in a significant way and his father had encouraged that idea not caring that it was a lie. The man had set her up for a broken heart at the very least. It could have turned out to be a horrible marriage that would have destroyed not only Moira but his own son. It was more important that Alex got his way than if his children were happy.

The man was a monstrous parent and when he was gone there would be so much chance for happiness for both Lionel and Fiona. He should have felt guilty for wanting it to happen soon, but there was nothing left to love about the man. Lionel was tired of having to pick up the pieces of his sister's shattered heart when their father lashed out.

The sound of music behind him let him know that Lilith had begun her walk down the aisle towards him in the gown that Princess Elin had brought with her. Lionel took a deep breath, drinking in the stained glass that illuminated the sanctuary of the church, then turned his head to see Lilith. His heart stopped in his chest and his jaw almost dropped. The gown was dark blue, nearly sapphire, with silver detailing that shimmered with each step. Her long dark brown hair that he loved was coiled and bound around her head in a coronet.

Gone was the simple country maiden he had married in the field and in her place was a princess that belonged in the court of Camelot. If he had ever doubted that Lilith could walk among the royalty and nobility of the court those thoughts were washed away. This woman, his woman, could stand with the Queen herself and any man would be hard pressed to tell the difference between them.

"That is the scullery maid you married?" Prince Banning whispered in his ear. "There were never maids as lovely as that when I was growing up."

"Are you sure about that? Perhaps you did not see them because they were maids?" Lionel replied, stepping down to meet Lilith at the foot of the alter.

If the prince answered him Lionel did not hear it. His eyes were fixed on his beautiful wife. After this he would be able to boast to the world that he had the most beautiful wife in all the kingdom. He was so mesmerized by her elegance and beauty that he barely heard the words and instructions of the priest. After Lilith gave the priest her answer with a beaming smile upon her face that told Lionel that she shared his joy he thought that perhaps he had been overly concerned about Moira. That was until he heard her voice called from the bottom of the steps.

"This wedding cannot proceed Father Ignatius." She called loudly up to the priest who was trying to hide a smug smile.

"Why is that my child?" Ignatius said, just as loudly. It was as though he knew the answer and wanted it broadcast for all to hear.

"Lionel cannot marry Lilith because he laid with me first and even though I told him that I wanted to marry him he refused. He cannot marry another woman when he took my virtue and refused to do the honorable thing." Moira helped Sir Alex to his feet beside. "His father knew this and told me that he would ensure that his son did the right thing."

Lionel's eyes moved from the priest to his wife to the pair at the bottom of the stairs. How could his own father do this to him when he had done everything he had asked? How could he do this to Lilith who had never done anything to hurt or offend him?

His eyes flew to her face.

Lilith looked appalled. The joy that had been on her face moments before was gone, replaced with horror and distrust.

"How could you not tell me that you had been her first?" Lilith said. "I knew that she had flirted with you since you returned and boasted about how she was your first, but how could you do that and not marry her? What if she had become pregnant? What would you have done then? Would you have left her as I was left?"

"Lilith it was not like that." He stammered, holding up a hand to her. Where was Saffir with the druid? He could handle either of these attacks, but he could not deal with both, not without help. "I was not the first man that she was with and she never brought up marriage until I returned, years later. I swear it."

"How can I believe you? What about the promises you made to me in the dark of the night after you brought me to your bed? Were those the same that you made to her in order to get what you wanted?" Lilith cried, her voice choking on the tears that were gathering in her eyes at his betrayal.

He felt trapped, stuck, in the great hall of Scotsbane. It might have a ceiling like the church cathedral and be broad enough for dinner and dancing, but he felt as though he could not breath.

"I did not make those promises lightly, Lilith. I made them to you as my wife." Lionel said, reaching for her arm. "I intend to keep them, to you and to Elaine."

"No. You do not get to touch me." She jerked her arm out of his hold and clenched her fist, ready to strike if he tried to grab her again. "You never get to touch me again. I thought that you were different, that what we had was different. I was wrong. You are just like him, Elaine's father. How can you be so cruel? To marry me, make love to me when you are already spoken for? It would have been better to leave me alone to hide in the shadows. At least I have friends there of my own station."

He was shaking his head, staring at the ground, but his body was wracked with frustration and anger at Moira. A glance in her direction showed her to be delighted at the trouble she had caused.

"There is no where that you could go or hide that I would not see you." He took a slow step towards her, holding up his hands in a gesture of peace. "You have the eyes of an angel, the face a divine goddess and the body of magical temptress. Even if you were to join the sisters of the new religion you would stand out as unique, special. I do not want Moira. I never did. I want you, only you."

He watched her face. Watched her weigh her opinion of his words, decide if she could trust him or not. The chapel was so quiet that he could hear his father wheezing beside Moira. Everyone was waiting on what Lilith would say next. Lionel's entire world hinged on her decision. He would never marry Moira. There was no force on earth that could force him to do that.

If Lilith rejected him here and now he would hold her to the vows they made in the field yesterday and spend the rest of his life trying to win her back. He would abandon every other quest and calling until she once again smiled at him the way she had that morning. He needed her beside him to feel complete, to feel happy, to feel loved. He loved her. Why had he not realized that before now? It had taken the threat of losing her to make him see it.

"Lilith, I love you." He said it aloud and it felt incredibly right. "I did not understand it before now, but I love you. You are my friend, my lover, my wife. I love you."

The hurt and rage began to melt from her face at his words. He might not lose her after all. He took her hand and dropped to a knee. His eyes searched her face, silently pleading for the response that would not break his heart.

"How sweet. It does not matter though." Moira said, coming up the stairs. "He was mine first and I intend to hold him to the laws that command him to marry me after he takes my virginity. Perhaps one of the brothels in Camelot would take you on. That is, if you can do something about your bastard."

The sound of a slap echoed in the chapel. Princess Elin had done for him what he could not ever do himself. Physically stopped Moira from speaking out of turn again.

"Moira is right. I do not want the bastard of another man and a loose woman to inherit my household." Sir Alex said, pulling Lionel's attention to the bottom of the stairs. "I told her that Lionel would do the right thing by her. That his honor as a knight would never let him violate a woman and not see to her well-being afterwards."

"I did not take it. You know that and so do I, Moira. Find someone else." Lionel said, not taking his eyes from Lilith's face. "I am not going to marry her, father. I am taken."

"You do not have the power to set aside the law, Lionel." Father Ignatius said, his voice dripping with arrogance. "Since this ceremony is not finished, you have not been pronounced man and wife. Lilith is not your wife. You are not married."

"I think I can override your words, priest." Banning said, rushing up the stairs to face off against the man in the elaborate robe. "Want to push your church rules against the word of a crown prince?"

"Kings are ordained by God, and as such they can override the laws of man. You, however, are not a king yet Prince Banning." Father Ignatius said firmly. "You have no power here."

"The boy may have no power, yet, Ignatius but I have more than you ever will." The voice of Merlin boomed from the doorway. "So do the old gods who gave their blessing to this union yesterday at midday. The union of Lionel and Lilith has been completed, blessed by the gods of Briton through my hands, by the high king of Briton through my words and consecrated in body last night. Your tricks and manipulations are powerless against the past."

The druid strode firmly down the aisle with a power and ease that belied his age with Saffir behind him. He breezed past Sir Alex and Moira and climbed the step to stand opposite Banning and face down the priest.

"Do you wish a battle of wills with me, man of god?" The druid said with all the confidence in the world shining in his eyes. "I do not think so. Walk away and let the children make their own choices. You and yours have lost this round."

He turned to look down and Lionel and Lilith, the light pouring through the stained glass casing a blue halo around his head.

"Do not turn from love so quickly Lilith. Search your heart and let it guide you. It will not steer you wrong."

Lionel turned to look at his bride, feeling hopeful after the words of the druid.

"Lilith? What say you?"

"I say..." Lilith said with a serious frown, looking around the room. "That all of you men talk too much."

She turned to lock her eyes with Lionel's and smiled slowly.

"It hurts that you did this, and I will not pretend that it does not. I know you though and you are a good man. I saw you defend Elaine, protect her from those priests. You did not have to do that. It showed your heart and it stole mine. Of course, I love you Lionel."

She leaned up to kiss him, sliding her hands around his waist and pulling him closer.

Lionel responded by wrapping his arms around her and pulling her close. He wanted to devour her then and there, but that would have to wait until tonight. Tonight, and every night for the rest of their lives.

"Will you come home with me Lilith? Home to Redbourne?" He held out his hand to his wife.

"Yes, Lionel. Take me home so that we can give Elaine and the children of our future a home of warmth and love that is not haunted by the memories of our painful pasts. We will have a new beginning together." Lilith said, taking his hand and descending the stairs.

They walked past Moira and Sir Alex with Gerard, Saffir and the royal twins attending behind them. Merlin maintained his position at the top of the stairs, watching them go while the priests cowered away from him and his savage magic.

"We will. Redbourne is a place without judgement where love is allowed to grow. You will see when we arrive. Elin and Banning are coming with us and I think that you and Caelia will have more in common than the obvious."

"The obvious?" She asked with a confused smile. "What do we have in common that so obvious?"

"You are strong enough to love a knight."

Continued In "The Red Knight"

Epilogue:

The ride South from Scotsbane, with the royal twins as well as his sister, new stepdaughter, and his wife, had been so much more enjoyable than the journey North. Lionel had not cared that the wagon holding the ladies had slowed them to half of their previous pace. The company and conversation had been so much lighter, so much more pleasurable than it had been only a few days before. Elin, Fiona, and Lilith all got along, and the wagon overflowed with their joy and laughter. Little Elaine seemed to have fallen in love with Saffir and insisted on riding with him as often as she could gain permission to do so. The company of Prince Banning transformed the surly Gerard into a man full of so much joy he was practically boyish.

Joy and laughter were their constant companions.

Lionel could not remember a happier time in all his life.

Even the appearance of Lancelot and Sir Gawain when they neared Camelot did not have the power to dampen his mood.

"You have gone against the wishes of the King, young Lionel." Lancelot said, casting his eyes around their party. "He had thought that allowing Merlin to attend and perform the ceremony for you would be enough to convince you to stay at Scotsbane and do your duty."

"You can tell the king that I have managed to accomplish all he required that I do. I have taken a wife, a beautiful wife, of the old religion. I have made what peace I can with my father and have no further need to break words with the man in this life."

"What about the management of the estate? Keeping it out of the hands of the priests? Gawain asked. "That was the most important part. We cannot let them get more property."

Prince Banning and Gerard joined the conversation by bringing their horses to flank Lionel and show their support.

"That business was taken care of by the wedding." Banning said. "The papers were signed that when the time comes, and Sir Alex is deceased the property passes to Lionel and then his sister if he does not have an heir when he dies."

"His sister will have to marry for that legality to take place." Sir Lancelot said, flashing a smile towards the wagon of women. "I would hurry up and see that done quickly Lionel."

"She will marry who and when she chooses." Lionel said, shaking his head at the men from Camelot. Not even their pressure could taint the joy in freedom he was feeling. "Now, if you can excuse us, I would like to get my wife and daughter home so that I may introduce them to Sir Liam and get on with our lives which were so rudely delayed by the folly and foolishness of my father. We bid you gentlemen good-day and send our highest regards to the king."

Lionel turned his horse and led the group away from the senior knights. They were only a few days from Redbourne now and he was eager to get home. He wanted to show off his family and start the new life he had promised them. There would be so much happiness for all of them now. His sister would be able to marry for love and there would be no one whispering about Lilith and Elaine. Lionel could join the other knights in the hunt for Bedver, the man who had been behind Liam being removed from Camelot and who had kidnapped Caelia with the intent to frame Liam for her murder.

There was so much to be finished, so much to be started. Sharing a smile with his wife he thought of something else that they were eager to start.

The rest of the journey was filled with plans for the future during the day and plans for dealing with Bedver and the priests in the night. The errant knight would be dealt with as soon as possible. It was likely that it would be a violent encounter. He was known for having other men do his dirty work, so they had to be prepared for tricks and surprise attacks. They could deal with the greed of the priests after the villain was brought to justice.

It was just past midday on the twelfth day after they left Scotsbane that the group rode past the inn where Lionel had shared a tryst with Daisy. They were almost home and, since Camelot, there had been no disruption to their journey. Lionel hoped that there would be no need to stop and risk an encounter between Lilith and the last woman he had been with before her.

Though he had done nothing wrong the knight doubted that his wife would enjoy having her new husband's past dalliances thrown in her face so soon in their marriage. Lionel was riding beside the wagon and holding Lilith's hand while telling her about the area and listening to her as they rolled past. He was pressing a kiss to Lilith's palm when Daisy stepped out of the inn doorway.

"Be careful with that one, Miss." Daisy called, with a deep frown. "Sir Lionel is one of those types to love you and leave you in the morning. Have a care for your virtue."

"I think you will find that my husband is a man of honor with no further need of such services as you provide." Lilith replied in a confident sing-song voice. "I think you unwise to brag about such things so loudly when you have nothing to show for it."

"You handled that well." Lionel said to her, offering a smile. "I am sorry for that though. There will not be any others like that I swear. I have not courted anyone at Redbourne or had a regular lover. There are no more nasty surprises waiting for us."

He hoped that he was right. There was nothing he could think of that would or could be upsetting unless they did not like Redbourne. He would have to find a cottage for them. The rooms he occupied in the main house as a bachelor knight would only be acceptable for a short-term home. Lilith deserved to be the mistress of her own house at last, even if it was a small house.

His mind was still on the interaction at the inn the next day when they crested the hill that overlooked Redbourne. It was good to be home at last.

"Who is that waiting for us?" Elaine said, standing up in the wagon and pointing towards the broad-shouldered man astride a horse, waiting at the gate.

"I believe that is Sir Liam himself waiting to welcome us home." Gerard said, looking at Lionel. "You should ride up and meet him. Let him know that we have brought home more than anticipated."

"Right. Good idea." Lionel said, nodding to Gerard and offering Lilith and Elain a happy smile. "He is sure to be excited for us."

He dug in his heels and rode to meet his commander, grinning happily. His heart was full to bursting in that moment, nothing in the world could change that.

"Sir Liam. It is good to be home." He said, pulling up in front of the Silver Knight.

"It is good to have you back Lionel. Bedver has been making trouble again. It seems that he has teamed up with the church and is hunting those of the old religion. They are trying to make criminals of us all." Liam said with a frown. He held out a scroll and his expression changed to one of compassion. "Congratulations on your marriage. I wish that I had better news waiting for you to come home to, but this cannot be helped."

"Chasing down Bedver and some priests is hardly a disappointment Liam." Lionel said, chuckled as he unfurled the scroll and began to scan the unfamiliar writing. "How did you know that I was married? Ah, it is here in the letter. It also says…"

Lionel dropped the paper and as it fell to the ground he looked up at Liam. "My father is dead."